S0-AAC-524

OUR
CROZE
NEST

OUR
CROZE
NEST

A Morning River Farm Story

JOHN
GOULD

BLACKBERRY BOOKS

Copyright © 1997 by John Gould
All Rights Reserved

ISBN 0-942396-79-0
Blackberry Books, 617 East Neck Road,
Nobleboro, Maine 04555

Book Design
Christopher Smith

Cover Painting
Margaret Leonard

Author Photo
Peter Main

Drawing
Monica Griffiths

First Edition

Printed in the United States of America
Thomson-Shore, Dexter, Michigan

BOOKS BY JOHN GOULD

New England Town Meeting
Pre-natal Care for Fathers
Farmer Takes a Wife
The House That Jacob Built
And One to Grow On
Neither Hay nor Grass
Monstrous Depravity
The Parables of Peter Partout
You Should Start Sooner
Last One In
Europe on Saturday Night
The Jonesport Raffle
Twelve Grindstones
The Shag Bag
Glass Eyes by the Bottle
This Trifling Distinction
Next Time Around
No Other Place
Stitch in Time
The Wine of Pentagoet
Old Hundredth
There Goes Maine!
Funny About That
It Is Not Now
Dispatches from Maine—1942-1992
Maine's Golden Road
Our Croze Nest

With F. Wenderoth Saunders
The Fastest Hound Dog in the State of Maine

With Lillian Ross
Maine Lingo

Dedication

To remember Martha B. Lord of Denmark, Maine
Just "Pat" to us all

February 7, 1937   -   July 1, 1995

THE TRILOGY OF
MORNING RIVER FARM

This belated episode completes the trilogy of Morning River Farm, stories of far down east on the coast of Maine. The young man who relates the story explains the delay by saying he had to wait to see how it came out. *No Other Place*, the first of the three volumes, told how Jabez and Martha Knight came to make a home in colonial days "halfway between French and English." That is, between New France and New England. It tells how they were joined by Jules and Marie-Paule Marcoux, from Nova Scotia, and how the two couples lived together in peace and prosperity in the midst of political turbulence. The second volume, *The Wines of Pentagoët*, pursues the generation of Elzada, daughter of Jabez and Martha, who was beautiful, wealthy, bilingual, and gracious. She introduced flip to the Maine coast, a beverage more elegant than calibogus, which had hitherto been staple. Manny the Portagee then lived on Razor Island, and smuggled with Father Hermidore, a Jesuit based on the Magdalen Islands in the Gulf of St. Lawrence. Father Hermidore came to Maine to marry the lovely Elzada to her sea-captain friend, Lieutenant Alonzo Plaice, once of HMN but now a coaster of much knowledge and many interests. An amusing scene develops when Elzada simultaneously translates the French wedding ceremony into English for the bridegroom, who doesn't understand French.

The second of the trilogy also explains the miracle of the noble wines of Pentagoet, which were turned from Bordeaux quality to salt sea water between Bagaduce and Boston, causing anguish in Boston.

Our third story brings us into today, when summer people have discovered Down East. Please meet Cousin Snood half way. He'll go the other half gladly, and you can honk Monhegan-Island style.

Chapter 1

WHAT MY
FATHER BOUGHT

My father was what Maine coastal people call a ritch bitch, and he was irrevocably "from away." In Maine, anybody who lives farther from the ocean than you do is a highlander, so little more than four or five miles is enough to make "away," but my father was all the way from Philadelphia, the city of brotherly love, and he was a lawyer. He was also a good lawyer, and had practiced but a few years when he became general counsel for the Pennsylvania Railroad, a position he would hold until retirement and a position he already held when he first heard about Morning River Farm in Maine and laid down the check to buy it. My father was, if you please, loaded, and he qualified in every respect as a dubious person in the eyes of those Maine people who cherish their birthrights and are maybe a bit cross-eyed from looking down their noses. It was his railroad connection that took my father to Maine, a state he hitherto knew nothing about.

There had been, in the early dreams of transcontinental railroading, a proposal to link the prairie states, and even the Pacific coast, to the seaports of Maine, and while that proposal came to be called The Great North American and European Railroad, no tracks were laid and the dream fizzled. But some easements had been acquired and some track rights established, and the Pennsylvania Railroad wondered if these assets might be picked up for future reference. My father was one of the committee sent up to Maine to find out. And while in Maine he was told about Morning River Farm, a dreamland paradise that could be had for a song. They told my father nobody was interested because nobody really knew just where the place was, and as there were no roads you couldn't get there. They told my father there was shore property and timberland, all kinds of buildings, and at least five hundred acres of beautiful meadow farm land within the horseshoe bend of the river. At that time Maine hadn't put out signs to welcome tourists, and while there were some oceanside vacation resorts, and a few more on wilderness lakes, there wasn't a motel in the state, and the "summer complaint" hadn't moved in. Activity was beginning in Bar Harbor and Ogunquit, but I guess nobody had yet called the Rockefellers ritch bitches. The stories told about Morning River Farm beguiled my father, and while he decided the Great North American and European Railroad had nothing the Pennsy Road needed, he wanted to own Morning River Farm. He bought it sight unseen, although he did search the title at three court house registries, and then he asked somebody how to go about getting there.

He visited the place once by way of Monhegan Island, where he met Mr. Sherman Thomas, a lobster fisherman, and arranged for Mr. Thomas to become our caretaker. Mr. Thomas took him in his boat to the property and he got a very quick look at what he'd bought before he came home to break the glad news to my mother and me. My mother was not averse to social prominence, and to her social circle she let it be known we had seasonal property in Maine and the *Bulletin* dutifully put it on record. I was still seven years old, so didn't suppose I was now considered wealthy, a ritch bitch. I have an idea my father didn't tell anybody. So the winter passed, and in May we got ready to go to Maine and see our place at the seashore and to pass the first of many happy summers.

There were two dwellings; the big Jabez Knight farmhouse which Jabez built for his bride, Martha, and which in the next generation was the home of their daughter Elzada and her sea-captain husband, Alonzo Plaice. Then the smaller home built by Jules Marcoux, which was Normandy style. The five hundred acres of meadow within the horseshoe bend of Morning River made a dooryard for these two homes, and beyond the bend of the river, the hardwood growth made the horizon beyond which, somewhere, was the wilderness of the Maine forests. To the east, of course, was the Atlantic Ocean. It took quite some time to explore the sawmill, with its storage space, boat shop, and barrel mill. The wharf had a baithouse and a derrick. The several privies lost their importance when my father got a generator and put in plumbing. There was a stable for cows, horses, pigs, and sheep, and behind the Marcoux home a henhouse. We had a smokehouse. And it was after our third summer that Mr. Thomas, hunting woodcock in the fall, found the maple sugar house we didn't know we had. It was up on the hill beyond the bend in Morning River, amongst the sugar maple grove, and it had evaporation cauldrons on stone arches, a great many sap buckets stacked for storage, and a sugaring-off pan. The roof had weathered and rain had got in, so some things were spoiled. We never made repairs, since we were never there for sugaring season in March and April, so after a few years the building collapsed. But we had a sugar house!

And we also had everything the folks who lived in both houses had acquired in over two hundred years of living; not only the things they'd made but the things that they bought and had come by boat. The big house was full of books, which we came to call Elzada's library. Both houses had drawers and closets of dishes. We had garden tools, a room in the barn for slaughtering. We kept finding things. It was a long time before we knew what my father had bought. And now I've forgotten the forge and the anvil, and the complete smithy under the bucket shop. Even the sling to hoist an ox while his shoes were nailed on. Did you know an ox won't stand on three legs, as will a horse? Pick up his fourth hoof, and he'll fall down.

So on those beautiful June days when we were first at Morning River Farm, Miss Han, the daughter of Mr. and Mrs. Thomas, and I began exploring what my father had bought.

Chapter 2

OUR TWO FAMILIES

Cousin Snood insisted there is no substitute for blind luck, and my father's finding Mr. Thomas proves that. On his first visit to Morning River Farm, my father had sought help from the postmaster at Tenants Harbor, and he had suggested Sherman Thomas. Mr. Thomas was, as much as anybody, the local historian, and he still fished for lobsters from a sailboat. This time of year Mr. Thomas would be at his home on Monhegan Island, and it would be worth the price of a round-trip on the mail boat to talk with him. That was my father's lucky day. He not only persuaded Mr. Thomas to become our care-taker and handyman, to live during the summer in the Marcoux house, but he secured for us a true down-Maine lobster catcher to regale us with history and lore, fact and fancy, and wean us somewhat from the odious mishap of being from away. Most important, he knew as much as there was to know about Jabez and Martha, Elzada and Cap'n 'Lon, and the fabulous Jules and Marie-Paule Marcoux. He also told us stories about Manny the Portagee, about Father Hermidore, the Baron Castine, and other notables, French and English, who visited Morning River Farm in the long ago. Han had heard all his stories before, and now and then she'd kick me on the ankle and say, "Oh, this is a good one; now, get ready!"

Mrs. Thomas was pretty, although at seven going-on eight I wasn't all that much interested in women's looks. She was just fifteen years older than her daughter, and later the daughter would tell me she was "unexpected." More than that, my father would warn me, years later, not to let some scheming female set me up the way Mrs. Thomas hooked Mr. Thomas. Mrs. Thomas was an excellent cook and housekeeper, and had brought Han up to be as good. So that was one of the two families that came to Morning River Farm the first of June and stayed through August. Did I say that their daughter Han, short for Johanna, was three days younger than I? She was, and we grew up together, summer by summer, inseparable playmates. The Thomases stayed at Morning River to see us safely off to Philadelphia on Labor Day, and then returned to their own home out on Monhegan Island where Han would go back to school.

My father had a law office and staff, and also a side business as a labor arbitrator, but had no associate attorneys and did his railroad law work from the one office. After he acquired Morning River Farm he laid down a Golden Rule that was never to be violated: Under no circumstances was his vacation in Maine subject to intrusion by his legal work. If the president, he said, wants me for the Supreme Court, I'm not to be disturbed until the Senate confirms. He did little reading at Morning River, never fished or sailed, said the water was too cold for swimming, and wouldn't exercise except to walk with my mother twice around the house or once up and down the beach. My mother painted. I suppose my father had no illusions about her talent, but he indulged her by paying the sometimes large bills at the artists' supply store, and if he liked something she did he'd have it framed and find a place for it. My mother attended art seminars and went to gallery showings, and had had some showings herself. The *Bulletin* was generous to her, and would send the society photographer for a "head and shoulders." Then myself, and that was our family except for Mrs. Crowthers, our cook and housekeeper. At first, we thought Mrs. Crowthers would not go to Maine with us, and that Mrs. Thomas would be our cook. My mother never cooked anything. And Mrs. Crowthers swore she'd never go to Maine if her life depended on it, and if she did she would never cook a fish or any other of those awful things the people eat up there. She was petrified of boats and trains, and detested all fish. She favored street lamps. She was a widow, and had been hired to live with us before my mother and father were married. She changed my first didie, and I still remember bruising claps she gave to my dear little bottom when I needed some, although I have no recollections of why I was being punished. It would be nice if I could say I loved her, but my feeling is more that of awe and respect and in some ways she was a tyrant. But thoughts of a summer alone in the Philadelphia house changed her mind, and she found she loved the train ride once she got aboard and had a seat, but she never did boil, fry, bake, and stew any kind of a fish, although sometimes she would help Mrs. Thomas with her clam cakes and crabmeat cakes. Mrs. Crowthers did make an incomparable shepherds' pie.

The departed husband of Mrs. Crowthers had been a lawyer that my father knew professionally, but I think he never got beyond writing wills and drafting deeds. Mrs. Crowthers always dignified his memory by referring to him as, "The judge, my former." It's possible some might say Mrs. Crowthers "took over" and ran our household, and maybe she did, but she did it tactfully and we didn't notice. She certainly was dedicated to us and the last thing she would ever do would be to offend us in the congenial tyranny she practiced. My father loved her humor, and often said he'd buy her a red wig if she wanted to go on the stage.

Chapter 3

MR. THOMAS'S SLOOP

Mr. Thomas continued to fish for lobsters with his sailboat after everybody else had begun using power boats, and while he pleaded sentiment it was nothing of the sort. I've got to explain the Monhegan Island situation, because I never did get to haul lobster traps with Mr. Thomas, or anybody else. Monhegan has a lobstering season that differs from that on the rest of the Maine coast. The fishermen there all start on the same day, January first, and they make a ceremony of it. Everybody starts at the same time, and if for any reason a man isn't ready, the others wait for him, or even set his traps for him. The season then runs through the 31st of May; on June 1 the traps are all on the beach. Mr. Thomas was the only Monhegan Islander still fishing with a sailboat, but the reason was that he took summer folks on day sails, and also on clam bakes, much better under sail. My father didn't know about this when he asked Mr. Thomas to be his handy man at Morning River, and actually told me he hoped when I got bigger I could go out with Mr. Thomas to haul for lobsters, telling me to heed the man's wisdom and knowledge, and take advantage of all the things he could teach me. But we came each year the first of June and went back to Philadelphia on Labor Day.

Not right away, but after a few years I did get to sail with Mr. Thomas as a "hand," or as he called me, his "sternman." In lobstering, sometimes the owner of a boat will have a partner who goes with him and shares in the profits. It was Han who explained this to me. No Maine lobsterman cares to be "second fiddle," so the two "go snacks." That's share-and-share-alike. Mr. Thomas told my father there had been one year after Congress passed the income tax law that the government boys worked themselves into a tizzy over nothing at all.

Knowing nothing about down-east Maine customs and habits, the tax collectors insisted that if there are two men in a boat one of them is the boss and the other is an employee. Tax returns must be filed accordingly. How else would you do it? Everybody got audited and everybody was in trouble. But Maine lobstermen are independent minded and they like to work for themselves. So instead of being a hired hand, the second man went as a "sternman" and that's happily much different. It took some time to get this through the Washington lunkheads, and meantime a lot of Maine lobster catchers faced a stretch in the pen. And ten thousand dollars fine. But because of the Monhegan season, I never went sternman with Mr. Thomas, although he called me his sternman when I got big enough to help him some with the sloop.

Now, what about, Han? That first summer, I learned quickly what Mr. Thomas had known all along, namely; Han was a girl. No doubt others noticed it. Mr. Thomas had reconciled himself that Han wasn't going to have a brother, and thus he would lack a boy-child and have nobody in the family, when the time came, to be his sternman. Han knew everything there was to know about catching lobsters, and was no doubt willing, but it wasn't the same. Early on, Mr. Thomas said to me, "Be nice to have a boy around!" I didn't pay that much attention at the time.

Even though Mr. Thomas didn't haul while we were in Maine, I did get to know something about the sloop from him— and from Han. When he'd come in from one of his day sails or

17

a clam bake, he'd lay his sloop up to our wharf in a gentle caress, and Han and I would be there to make her fast and clean her. Han had been doing this, and didn't need much time to show me how. In the spring, out on the island, she'd help her father clean the sloop, washing down the boards and making everything ready for the night and for tomorrow. Sometimes there'd be a broken trap to repair, and Mr. Thomas would do that in his baithouse while Han tidied the sloop. She told me cleaning up after a sailing party lacked the great pleasure of filling the bait tub, but otherwise it was surprising how a half dozen summer people could dirty up a boat in one afternoon. Seashells, she said, frosted her tail good and plenty. Everybody would roam the beach and pick seashells, and then leave them on the sloop, usually tucked under a cushion where it would be easy to find them in a day or so. A handful of good winkles, she said, would ripen in almost no time at all, and a starfish was a great deal better. When she got through, and then when *we* got through, the sloop was bright and clean, and ready for another clam bake tomorrow. Then we'd double check the lines, so the sloop was secure for the night, and go for a swim. Mr. Thomas had enough of a "sternman" in Han so he never checked her in this, and he never checked me out, either.

By the time Han and I had dried off, Mr. Thomas was ready for "The Big Surprise," which was "What's for supper?" He put in long days, both at lobstering and at his party sails. He picked and chose some, so he didn't take summercaters every day, but kept time to do this and that as his Morning River work. And when he was available I followed my father's suggestion and stayed close to his heels. Most of the time, that's where Han would be, too, and I was glad about that.

Mr. Thomas told my father, and I listened, that his great love for his sloop wasn't all poetry. He said it wasn't too long ago, but before his time, that everybody lobstered from a sloop, which was the traditional work boat of Maine. He said after the Pilgrims had been down in Massachusetts a year or so they were hungry, and they sent their own little sloop down to Maine to see if they might cadge a little something more tasty than clams. Clams, day after day, had a way of lingering that annoyed the pious Pilgrim in the pursuit of his unalienable rights. The Pilgrims did sail up to the Damariscove Islands, and their journal tells how astonished they were to find Maine well populated and busy. Sloops, the journal says, were going and coming, flitting about the islands. Mr. Thomas said, "Until then, the Pilgrims thought America was like Heaven. Nobody was here except Pilgrims." Mr. Thomas added, "For sure, the Pilgrims didn't know that all these people on the Maine Coast went home on Labor Day! Which in a way they did. They came in the spring and put in gardens, fished all summer, and moved off when it got cold. Not a few of them went to England until L-Y time again. But they did load the Pilgrim sloop with groceries, and the Pilgrims went back to Massachusetts to survive and get important. They wrote in their book that these kind Maine folks wouldn't take any money for all the goodies, and that doesn't sound like anybody we have around here now. But these Maine people were doing what they were told to do. Seems the company in England wrote to their people in Maine, saying the Pilgrims were on the way, that they were a quirky sort and not to plague 'em, and if they needed help to do the right thing. You can look that up."

Mr. Thomas said, "From the first, a sloop was the right way to do things in these parts."

When a summer moon fulled, Han and I would walk down to the wharf and sit on the sloop. The sloop's stern to the west, the rising moon over the bowsprit, Han and I would just sit there and wait to get sleepy.

A sloop is a good thing to have in your life.

Chapter 4

THE FLIP
HOUR

Han told me fairly soon that her father always kept a bottle of Black Diamond rum in the cuddy of his sloop, and it was a Monhegan Island custom of lobster catchers, when they met at sea, to reach across and hold each other's boats by the coaming and have a "honk" while they drifted. I thought, of course, of two fishermen making a noise like a gaggle of geese, but Han set me right. A honk is a ceremonial swig from the mouth of a "jug," preferably of Black Diamond rum, for any reason or for no reason, and if a Maine fisherman is invited to honk the acceptable reply is, "Don't mind if I do; it does get some old dry out here, don't it?" I was to learn that honking is also honored in the breach, but Cousin Snood told me honking dissenters are hard to find on any given day of the week.

In the beginning, after my father bought Morning River Farm, he assumed that because Maine had a prohibition law nobody in Maine ever touched a drop, and while negotiating with Mr. Thomas about being our caretaker he was careful that the subject didn't come up. Mr. Thomas, likewise presuming, supposed Philadelphia people would abstain, and as a consequence nothing like a cocktail party materialized. When a jug of Black Diamond rum did show up at our notorious lanch of the sailing dory, my father thought it was probably an old lanch custom and didn't pursue it. My father was not abstemious. He and my mother had cocktails, but not every afternoon, and they were liberal enough to let me have a sip so I could feel "grown-up." It wasn't the rum or the "honk" that brought this contretemps to an end. It was flip.

There had been a rouser of a thunder clapper in the afternoon, and when we finished supper we walked down the wet path to sit on the Marcoux porch and have some popcorn Han had fixed. That was when my father asked Mr. Thomas why he paid his real estate taxes to the state rather than to a local government. In Philadelphia, he said, he got his tax bill from Philadelphia and he paid it in Philadelphia, but here in Maine he had to mail his check to Augusta and to the statehouse. Mr. Thomas grinned and said, "You'll find that we don't do a lot of things the way you do in Philadelphia. I'll do some thinking and draft a report, and I'll explain all that at a subsequent meeting." He said, "Good corn, Han!"

Han said, "There's more."

Then Mr. Thomas said, "I almost said, 'our next flip meeting.'" And when my father asked about a flip meeting, Mr. Thomas said, "Do you honk?"

My father said, "In Philadelphia? Certainly not!"

Mr. Thomas went ahead and told how Madam Elzada was famous for her Morning River flip, and in her time every visitor was handed a mug of flip when he stepped onto the wharf. Up to her time a calibogus was the important refreshment of the Maine coast, but she changed all that. I think it was then that my father asked what a flip is.

Mr. Thomas said Elzada was at a hotel in Boston one time and asked for a flip, and as the hotel didn't know what a flip was, she wrote the "reseet" out and showed how to make one. After that flip began to be served instead of a calibogus. One time, Mr. Thomas said, Elzada wrote her reseet in French, and they have it framed in the Harvard library. My father said he hoped he wasn't going to die of old age before somebody told him what the hell a flip is.

Mr. Thomas said for years Harvard had the reseet printed on penny post cards and sold copies to visitors for five dollars.

Mr. Thomas said to my father that he was coming to that, but the main thing was the flip sweetener. This was made in advance with eggs and cream, and sweetened with molasses or maple syrup, or in some places dried pumpkin seeds. At taverns, where flip was just what a dry and dusty traveler needed, some of the flip sweetener would be put in a mug and the mug filled with beer and rum, half-and-half, and then the mixture was stirred with the hot poker from the fireplace. I remember my father said, "And he asks me if I honk!"

Mrs. Thomas said she had Elzada's own reseet, but she hadn't made any flip sweetener in ages. She said there was Black Diamond on the sloop, and as soon as somebody got some of Cousin Snood's beer she'd have a flip hour like old times. Mr. Thomas said, "That'll make a good chance to tell you why you pay taxes to the state."

Mr. Thomas said that after Elzada caused flip to be the genteel social drink in these parts, the calibogus went out of style. He said the clergy always claimed the calibogus led to perdition, but the flip was considered somewhat elegant. Fact was, he said, that a minister who had the pulpit on Loud's Island took a flip with him to lend dignity to his Sunday sermon, and with a sip now and then he preached one of his best on the subject of the ten apostles and the twelve commandments. Mr. Thomas said it is historical that Elzada's flip caused the calibogus to fade into innocuous desuetude. Afterwards, my father said, "Right then, I swore an oath never-never to ask him what a calibogus is."

But my father was dedicated to his promise to keep Morning River Farm as much as he could the way it was when he found it, and to perpetuate its lore and traditions, so as lord of the manor he told Mrs. Thomas to start the sweetener and get word to Cousin Snood. Han was bringing in more popcorn, and she told my father, "You may like Elzada's flip; it always puts

Daddy to sleep."

And this was so. No matter how engrossed he was in one of his stories, and no matter how intensely we were listening to it, after his flip Mr. Thomas would come to the point where he said, simply enough, "Well, good night!" and he'd get up from his chair and head for bed. That was that. But I can add that at the next flip hour he would, sooner or later, say, "Well, to resume . . ." and he'd pick up where he had left off.

Our Morning River Farm flip hours were seminars of fact and fancy, with Professor Thomas at his lectern, and at the second or third and fourth, and perhaps part of the fifth, Mr. Thomas did explain why the taxes are paid at the statehouse.

Chapter 5

FLIP HOUR
GUESTS

The restoration of the Morning River flip hour was successful. Often, Han and I would miss it, as it came during our swim time. Since Mrs. Thomas made the flip sweetener and got things ready, we'd meet at the Marcoux house, including Mrs. Crowthers, who protested every time that she'd have just a small one. Mr. Thomas told us we should give a thought every afternoon to the way things were in the days of Elzada. The ocean was a highway, and almost any minute a boat of some size would be passing—a sloop doing some fishing, or a good-sized schooner headed for or coming from the West Indies. Morning River Farm was the only settlement on a long stretch of coast. Jabez and Jules repaired boats and built boats. Here was a place for every passing vessel to stop for at least a hail. If the folks at Morning River needed anything, tell a passing boat what to bring and it would arrive on the return trip. That's how Elzada got all her books. Everybody brought news. The big house did have rooms, but people passing spent the nights on their boats in a safe anchorage. The big thing was a flip! Mr. Thomas repeated the yarn about the black man on a coaster's crew who was proficient in rolling a full barrel of dark rum down a plank into the big house cellar, bringing it to a halt ready for the spigot. He'd get the barrel rolling and then steer it with one foot. He was the one who had his flip and then sang songs of Marseilles Harbor all evening with Jules and Marie-Paule Marcoux. Always just one flip.

So for years Morning River was the place for all traffic to pause, to have a flip and to pass the gossip. To wait for the tide. My father made his formal decree that the flip hour shall be revived and every session commence with a toast to Elzada. If Han and I were there, we'd join in— "To Elzada!"

There were days, plenty of them, during our Maine summers that a small blaze on the hearth would cheer the room, and the hot poker was no problem. Then one afternoon Mr. Thomas said, "I've just had a brainstorm!" and he left to walk over to his sloop. He brought back a blowtorch. There was some small job or other that needed a blowtorch and it got left on his sloop. He touched the thing off, and we had a new way to heat the flip poker.

Although Mrs. Crowthers always insisted one small flip was her limit, she'd make herself a second one shortly. My mother, who never had more than one small one, would giggle with Mrs. Crowthers about things nobody else considered funny. My father would discuss important matters with Mr. Thomas until he found Mr. Thomas had fallen asleep. Then Mrs. Crowthers would jump up with "My Goodness! The time!" and hurry up to the big house to fix supper. Except when we had fish. Mrs. Crowthers refused to cook fish, and on any fish evening we'd all stay for supper at the Marcoux house and Mrs. Thomas would serve. On fish nights Mrs. Crowthers would have another flip and help Mrs. Thomas.

There was one afternoon that Mrs. Thomas was going to boil lobsters, and Han and I were still at our Croze Nest when a schooner came in and tied up at our wharf. Curious, Han and I watched four people walk up to the Marcoux house, and in a few minutes we went over ourselves to find out who was calling. When we arrived, the four people had already joined the flip party, and were asking what this flip might be. Mr. Thomas explained it was a traditional beverage of the Morning River Farm, and all visitors were served flips as soon as they stepped ashore. One man asked about this Elzada person, and Mr. Thomas gave a flowery description at length. Han and I were introduced, when we came in, as a couple of poor children from up Bangor way, and Mrs. Thomas gave us both a very small flip with very little rum. The four visitors off the schooner stayed for lobsters and well after dark walked down to their boat to spend the night. By breakfast time, they were gone.

We never saw them again, and have no idea who they were. Except that my father insisted he knew. "The good-looking female," he said, "was Elzada!"

Chapter 6

MOTHER'S ART

My mother's artistic talent was never encouraged, but she was pleased to be considered gifted. As a young lady, she did go to Spain to be "appraised" by some artist of note, and came home again to be a housewife who "dabbled." Now and then the library would hang one of her efforts with a little sign that said "On loan from the artist." Nobody said so, but it was understood these paintings on loan could be bought, but none of hers was ever sold. The Philadelphia *Bulletin* sometimes printed one of these, but in the social pages rather than the cultural. My father would have one of her paintings framed now and then and it would hang in the house for a while. Then he, or my mother, would give it to somebody as a gift, and my father would have another framed. Even her husband and her only son, and not even my mother herself, had any illusions about her ability, but she had great enjoyment with dabbling. She did have a "studio" at home, but it was at Morning River Farm in the joy of summer that she let herself go. One day my father found a Harry Lauder Tam-o'-shanter in a golf shop and brought it home for my mother to wear as a beret. She, in turn, found a smock, and while her rocks always seemed to be floating on the water, she looked very like an artist. At Morning River she did some painting in the upstairs hallway, but she found the light there too bright and liked to paint in our Croze Nest. This didn't disturb Han and me, although the constant stink of turpentine wasn't pleasant. After we'd been at Morning River a few weeks, our Croze Nest had a collection of paintings leaning against the walls, which would be tied in a bundle come September for transport to Philadelphia.

There was very much a wry smile in what happened next. Nell Thomas, Han's mother, who was always outspoken about people "from away," and constantly deplored the exploitation of honest Maine people by summercaters and newcomers, decided my mother should have a gallery and offer her works to the public. At that time, Monhegan Island had already acquired its colony of summertime artists and this included painters who needed two or three tries to do a seagull. Compared to some of them, my mother would be good. Mrs. Thomas decided, and was by no means wrong, that little notes tacked up at the island post office would cause art lovers to swing over from Monhegan to visit a real, down-east Maine artist who painted in a boathouse and bucket shop. Mrs. Thomas also had Mr. Thomas make signs to go down by our estuary and point to the gallery. We did, occasionally, see a pleasure boat pass, either going to or coming from the Bar Harbor region, and some of them were good-sized craft. They turned out to have a fair share of art seekers, and playing her part well my mother entertained them in her smock and tam, and Mrs. Thomas did sell a few pictures.

Over on the seaward side of Razor Island there was a heronry in the spruce trees, and just about any time in the summer we could see at least one heron down the estuary, balanced on one leg and waiting for a fish to pass. Early on, my mother painted a picture of such a heron, his sword-like beak high in a posture of readiness. It was fun to bird-watch and see him spear a fish in a semi-twinkling of a flash and then sweep his wings and take off, satisfied for the moment. My mother painted one of them and caught the moment "in the life." The very next boat brought a customer, so my mother painted the same scene again, and after that always had a "shitpoke" drying in the corner and another canvas waiting to be adorned. Depending on how often visitors came to the gallery, Mrs. Thomas sold every Great Blue Heron my mother could turn out.

One afternoon Han and I had waited until my mother cleaned her brushes and had put her smock and tam on a hook and had left our Croze Nest, and I looked up to find Han all ready for the spillway pool, and nothing on but my mother's tam-o'-shanter, standing on one leg and holding out one arm like a beak.

Another subject my mother favored was the cascade pool by the back door of the big house, with a reflection in the pool. Also, she liked to paint the sloop of Mr. Thomas at our wharf, with a fishhawk perched on the masthead. When Mr. Thomas saw this one he said, "A painted osprey's all right, but shoot the damn real ones before they dump their gurry on the sloop!" Over the summers, Han and I washed off a lot of osprey manure and seagull dung, but my mother's birds never offended.

But that was the one and only season of my mother's artistry. Back in Philadelphia she intended to work that winter to build up an inventory and be ready for next summer. But a few days after we were home my father came from his office to ask my mother if she knew a gentleman named Kepler, "or some such name," and she said, "No, why?"

It seems Mr. Kepler had telephoned to ask my father if he might "meet the Maine artist?" He would stop by at the house early in the evening "if that is convenient." He did come, and as I was nearest I answered the doorbell. Mr. Kepler was a fine-looking man and carried a walking stick for show. He handed me a card and said he was expected. He introduced himself to my mother and my father as a dealer in art. He was aware of my mother's gallery in Maine, and was fortunate enough to have her canvas of The Great Blue Heron.

Mr. Kepler said he owned and operated eleven art stores, three in New Jersey, some in Maryland, and the others here in Pennsylvania. Would it be possible for him to become the sole outlet of Madam's paintings? He thought the time was right to introduce an authentic down-east lady artist. He hoped this would begin a long and happy relationship, and would it be convenient if his lawyer called to make whatever arrangements would be acceptable to Madam?" Then he added, "And to you, too, sir!"

My father touched his fingers together, his signal that he was in a judicial meditation, and he said, "I am, myself, an attorney, and I've just been in conference with my client about this very matter. I'll tell you how many oils and how many water colors, and how many are framed in white pine, and you tell me what you'll pay, cash in hand."

Mr. Kepler said, "Are these here or in Maine?"

"Some here; some in Maine. What do you expect your market will be for my wife's work?"

"Frankly, the once-in-a-lifetime buyer. Somebody who needs a pretty picture to cover a stain on the wall paper. A few of them may sell for calendar covers."

My father said thank you, and showed Mr. Kepler to the door. He said to Mr. Kepler, "I'll hear from you soon?"

"Right away. Good evening!"

Mr. Kepler came to Morning River the next summer, arriving in a power yacht with a crew of three. He picked up the paintings stored in the Croze Nest, including all the blue herons on one leg. He had already taken the paintings in our Philadelphia attic, including the blue herons standing on one leg. So Han and I got our Croze Nest back, and my mother began painting again just for fun. Mrs. Thomas closed the gallery and the smock and tam were retired to the coat hook on the wall. After we were all done with Mr. Kepler, my father waltzed my mother a couple of turns and said, "Welcome back into the family, gracious lady! I've been wondering how I was going to get you out of the clutches of that greedy down-Maine Thomas woman! You can paint all you please, but this Maine-coast artist stuff is a damned lie! To me, you just go back to being from away!"

Chapter 7

OUR CROZE NEST

Han named it, and our Croze Nest was our private hang-out, club room, secret place, headquarters and everything else. The Croze Nest became recognized as ours, and while anybody was welcome to open the door and walk in, nobody much did. Originally, the room, and it was sizable, was the cooperage and part of the sawmill. Han and I made a complete inspection of all the Morning River property during our first couple of weeks together, and until the others had done the same in more leisurely manner, we were the ones who knew just what we had. We found the sailing dory up on the timbers, and we found the mysteries of the bucket shop. From that moment on, anybody could have anything else, but Han and I owned that dory and we owned that room.

The bucket shop had been the cooperage. Mr. Thomas said the legends of Morning River had Jabez Knight and Jules Marcoux building and repairing boats, and farming, but the great need for barrels, or casks, in the area turned their attention to coopering as a very profitable sideline. For one thing, Morning River had considerable white oak timber. Since neither man had ever been instructed in the making of barrels, and since neither owned any cooper's tools, the business didn't start up right away.

It was believed that Jules went to Nova Scotia and worked one winter in a barrel factory, and then came back to teach Jabez. They had a very prosperous business from the start. Tight barrels, made for liquids, were in steady demand, not only for various fish products in brine, but for the so-called "West Indies Goods," molasses and rum for starters. Every northbound schooner bought rum, and every southbound schooner bought barrels. Then, with developing connection, there were sales to the vineyards of Europe. Then, the Morning River generations changed and all at once nobody made buckets, firkins, kegs, tubs, barrels, and casks. Han and I walked in and found the place just as it had been so long ago.

All the tools, special for coopering, were on the benches or hanging on wall pegs. All the special vises were there, attached to the walls or the benches. There was even a considerable pile of seasoned shook and lumber to shape more. And there were finished tubs and barrels in all sizes, two or three of each. There was one smaller tub, maybe fifteen or twenty of them, that Han and I wondered about, and Mr. Thomas didn't know what it was for. It was at least a couple of years before we found out; Cousin Snood, Mr. Thomas's cousin, said it was for collecting maple sap to make syrup. Han and I used one for a waste basket and for butternut shells.

One of the coopering tools on the bench was some kind of chisel, or gouge, that had adjustable guides, and seemed to have the handles in the wrong places. The cutter was very sharp and rounded. We tried to figure it out and couldn't, and then Mr. Thomas said he knew what it was for but couldn't remember the name. Later, he recollected and said it was for making the croze. He showed us on one of the barrels. Each stave of a barrel has a groove at each end, and when a cooper sets up the staves to make a barrel, the head and bottom fit into the croze grooves. He said the stave was held just so in a vise, and it took strong arms and know-how to cut the croze. Han and I tried it, but he was right. So Han began calling our bucket shop our Croze Nest. Not too many people ever came around to ask us why, but we showed the crozing tool to those who did.

Some summers later, when we got to know Cousin Snood better, he said some day he'd show us how to make a barrel, but he never found time to do it. He did tell us that one of the greatest skills in all shop work is to make the staves stand up when you cooper.

Han helped her mother some with housework and cooking, but she also kept our Croze Nest tidy. Before too long she got a mirror somewhere and drove a nail. There was a workbench in one corner and she found a pad that fit it. Not a mattress, but near enough. The bench became our "bunk-bed." She brought a blanket and a throw from the big house. And she always kept a vase of wild flowers on a shelf or on a table. Later, we moved the big telescope to our Croze Nest and whatever else we were doing at the time, we raced to the Croze Nest when any kind of boat appeared to be looked at.

Sometimes, on rainy days, we'd "borrow" a book from Elzada's library, and spend some time in the Croze Nest with it. We never took a book apiece, but would have just one and take turns reading to each other. Han was a better reader than I, and when she got tired telling me what the big words meant my father had his office in Philadelphia mail us a dictionary and I had to look things up myself. Han said, "It's funny; why wouldn't Lady Elzada have her own dictionary?"

There was the short time, and during just one summer, when my mother set up an easel in our Croze Nest and painted rather faithfully. That was the summer of the Great Blue Heron, who would fly over from Razor Island to pose. Whenever my mother was there painting, Han and I would move to another place in the sawmill or on pleasant days would go outside. Later, and sometimes, we'd go for a sail in our dory. Our Croze Nest had an importance we didn't care to share.

Chapter 8

THE CROZE
NEST WALL

My father couldn't jot down a telephone number unless he had his lawyer's pad of ruled yellow paper, and my mother always used the same for her grocery list or to write my teacher a note if I were about to be late. Mrs. Crowthers also got into the yellow paper habit. I presume that somewhere in our family keepsakes there is a sheet of lawyer's yellow paper with my first A-B-C's on it. So I was much puzzled the morning I found a poem on lawyer's paper tacked to our Croze Nest wall. I thought my father must have broken down and lost himself in the delight of the wing-ed word. Nothing of the sort, I was relieved. It was Han, who had found some verses she liked, and had copied them from the Elzada book for permanent display in the sanctified archives of the old bucket shop. As far as I know, the poem I read for the first time that morning is still tacked to the Croze Nest wall, and I think it more than possible that the words and thought John Milton gave to Mother Eve have not lost a thing in Han's heart after all these years. I made a copy for me afterwards, on a sheet of yellow lawyer's paper.

Without Thee

Sweet is the breath of morn, her rising sweet,
With charm of earliest Birds; pleasant the Sun
When first on this delightful Land he spreads
His orient beams, on herb trees, fruit, and flour,
Glistring with dew; fragrant the fertile earth
After soft showers; and sweet the coming on
Of grateful Evening milde, then silent Night
With this her solemn Bird and this fair Moon,
And these her Gemms of Heav'n, her starrie train:
But neither breath of Morn when she ascends
With charm of earliest Birds, nor rising Sun
On this delightful land, nor herb, fruit, flour,
Glistring with dew nor fragrance after showers,
Nor grateful evening mild, nor silent Night
With this her solemn Bird, nor walk by Moon,
Or glittering Starr-light without thee is sweet.

Chapter 9

ELZADA'S BOOKS

We called it "Elzada's Library," or more often "Elzada's Books," and for a couple of years we didn't think of it as the wonderful asset it was. The library just about filled the big house. All the bedrooms had been shelved, as had the main living room below, and the wide staircase going up from the front door was no more than steps between rows of books. As a family, which included Mrs. Crowthers, our cook, we were not bookish. My father did his reading in law books and journals, and vowed he would never read on vacation in Maine. My mother was a hobbyist in paints, and while her friends read books and belonged to reading clubs and supported the Philadelphia public library, my mother would open her water colors and do her own thing. I was too young, and Mrs. Crowthers had her fiction magazines.

But as time ran along we learned more and more about Elzada and the people who lived at Morning River Farm in the old days, and one beautiful summer evening we were sitting by the cascade pool, back of the house, and the sunset was magnificent. My father was moved to philosophize, and he started: "We don't spend enough time thinking what it was like here a hundred years ago. This Elzada. She wasn't exactly a backwoods woman deprived and ignorant. Sherm Thomas tells me she was extremely beautiful, that her gowns came from London and Paris, that she was rich, and that her ship-captain husband had more money than she did. Fact, Sherm says, that they kept their money in wine barrels down cellar, like potatoes and apples. When the cellar was full, they carried it up to the attic in clam hods." My father said this so we imagined Lady Elzada sitting here just the way we were, looking at the sunset—her own, private sunset. Except that Elzada had a book in hand.

"According to the stories, Elzada's father wanted to send her to school or college, which young ladies didn't get to do in those days, specially if they lived halfway to nowhere as she did. And Elzada struck a bargain with him about that. She said she didn't want to leave Morning River, and she'd educate herself right here in her own way. That's when they began buying books and building library shelves.

"Sherm tells me the ocean out here was full of boats in those days. Not only fishing boats, but all sorts of coasters going to the West Indies, from Newfoundland and all Canadian ports. There was what they called a mail cask moored off Razor Island, and every boat that went by stopped to leave or pick up, and Sherm says they had better mail service than they do now, and it didn't cost a cent. So Elzada and her Pa could get books from anywhere just by waiting for some boat to bring them, and there wasn't much else to do around here in those times except wait. Consequence was that Elzada did educate herself, and she built up the best—perhaps the *only*—library in Maine. Old Ben Franklin founded our Philadelphia library in 1732, and Sherm says Morning River Farm already had Elzada's books piling up before that. Makes you stop and think.

"Elzada was competent in two languages, and got books in both. And she turned out to be the gracious lady of diplomacy, bringing negotiators to her house here to settle problems. Sherm says if it hadn't been for Elzada, our Maine would belong to France and Canada today, and that she definitely kept this part of Maine for Massachusetts instead of letting it go to

New York. I was surprised that a lobster fisherman like Sherm Thomas would know as much as he does about the past.

There were several times after that when my father would repeat things Mr. Thomas had told him about Elzada and her books, and then a couple of things happened in the winter down in Philadelphia. First, somebody interested in Girard College came to call on my father about these books he'd bought up in Maine. My father had told about them to friends, and word ran around. This man suggested my father donate the Elzada books to Girard College. The second thing was that another man, having heard about the Elzada books, came to make an offer for them. This man had a second-hand book shop and called himself an antiquarian bookseller, and he was ready to pay cash and charter a boat that would go up to Maine with some experts who would catalog and pack the library. My father told these men that he would think things over, and he did decide that next summer he would look around and find somebody competent to spend some time at Morning River Farm and catalog Elzada's books and arrange them in good library fashion.

In the meantime, Han had somewhat taken over the Elzada books and had become possessive. At school, on Monhegan Island, Han had become teacher's helper with the books that came regularly from the state library. The township had to buy the usual classroom books, but for special studies the state would mail titles as requested by the teacher. And if anybody on the island wanted to read a certain book, new or old, he could ask the teacher to include it in the next shipment. Han kept track of all this, and unpacked the boxes when they came, re-packing them for return after use. And as Han worked with the teacher every now and then she would say, "We've got that one." She meant that the book on the list was also in Elzada's library. The teacher began to realize the extent of the shelves in our big house at Morning River.

And Han, having complete freedom with Elzada's books, came to know them all, and began to read them. She tried to get me excited about poetry, but that didn't work, and one day when we were after a mess of chowder cunners she repeated the names of all the bones in the human body. Oh, yes! Elzada had acquired professional books and her medical titles included anatomy as well as what-to-do-until-the-doctor-comes for both man and beast.

The next summer my father was telling about two chances he had to dispose of Elzada's books, and Han interrupted him with, "But you can't do that."

I suppose thinking like a lawyer my father would surmise he could do about as he pleased with his own property, so he turned to Han and said, "Oh? Young lady? Why not?"

Han said, "Because I ain't read 'em all yet."

There was never again the slightest thought that Elzada's books would be moved along.

Han never did read all the books. She and I filled our summers with other duties and pleasures, and in winter she was on the island and the books were on the main. She never took an Elzada book to the island. Now and then the state library wouldn't have a title, or a book on that subject, but Han could see it in her mind's eye right there on a bedroom, or staircase, shelf.

As Han would tell her teacher about Elzada's books, the teacher came to realize they made quite a library, and she expressed a wish to see the books. Mr. Thomas said he thought there would be no objection, but this wasn't something he'd do on his own. He wrote to my father, who liked the idea, and he suggested they pick a good day and the whole school could ride over in the sloop, visit the library, and have a mug up before the fireplace. Maybe Mrs. Thomas would make cookies and cocoa. And why didn't Han prepare a short speech on the history of Morning River Farm and why this library existed? This was done. Mr. Thomas wrote that he was lucky in choosing a sunny and warm day, and all went well. Mr. Thomas suggested the school send a thank-you note to Philadelphia, and when Han wrote it the teacher and all the scholars signed it. When the letter came to Philadelphia, I got so homesick for Maine my mother wondered if she should call a doctor. For days I was in the slump of what Han called a "pink stink" and dwelt miserably on my sad lot—why couldn't I be up there and going to school with Han?

Chapter 10

SLIVER UP
MY ARSE

"But what if something happens?" always bothered my mother and Mrs. Crowthers while at Morning River Farm, but Mrs. Thomas and her daughter Han didn't worry the same way. There was no physician and no health facility on Monhegan Island, so if something did happen that needed more than home remedies a "trip to the Main" was in order. Once at Morning River we didn't even have a boat other than the beautiful sloop of Mr. Thomas, and taking a toothache to a dentist in Rockland was a formidable challenge. In a way I eased the fear of my mother and Mrs. Crowthers early in our Morning River adventures, and I learned that modesty is adjustable. I'm guessing in recollection that it was the second week of our first summer at Morning River Farm. And early in the second week, because Han and I hadn't really become acquainted. I think we were still strangers, but working on it. Her mother was still just Han's mother and you can say I knew her only by sight. And what if something happens?

Whatever Han and I were doing, I slid along a plank and ran a splinter of spruce well into the cheek of my butt. The splinter went through the cloth of my cotton pants and broke off about a quarter of an inch from my skin. It didn't hurt at first, but when I moved the cloth moved the splinter, and I was transfixed in a very personal place with a pain that was long and hot. Han wanted to know if I was all right. Here was the finest opportunity to show my mother and Mrs. Crowthers what you do, way out here on the edge of the known world if something happens. Except that I had to tell Han first, and as new friends we were not practiced in discussing intimacies. Innovating, I said I'd run a splinter into my tail. Han said, "Where?"

Then Han and I became close friends. She well knew the Monhegan ways. My pants had been jerked down around my ankles, and Han was on her knees locating the splinter. She touched the end with a finger, and I knew I was mortally wounded and not long for this world. "Tickles, don't it?" she said. "Come on!"

Han grabbed up my pants, so I wouldn't try to run with the legs about my ankles, and holding them up she pushed me toward the Marcoux house. This wasn't good, so she said, "Wait!" and she pulled my pants off, greatly disturbing my personal splinter, and we arrived in the Marcoux kitchen where Mrs. Thomas was at the stove making something that smelled spicy and good. Han said, "Mom, he shoved a sliver up his arse!"

I underwent surgery.

By now the splinter hurt like the devil, but it hadn't bled but a drop. The wood had the hole plugged. I couldn't see it, but I felt, and Mrs. Thomas slapped my hand away and said, "If you pick it, it'll never heal." To Han she said, "Fishhook pliers is all, I guess."

While Han ran to the wharf to get pinchers from the sloop, Mrs. Thomas poured some hot water into a basin and opened some gauze she took from a cupboard. "I bet that smarts some wicked!" she said, and she told me to lie belly-down on the kitchen table. She barely touched the splinter and I yelled. "You gonna be spleeny?" she asked, and I knew I wasn't about to cry out again. Han came in with a murderous-looking pair of heavy pliers, which Mrs. Thomas stuck in the pan of hot water. She patted my unwounded cheek very friendly-like, and said,

"Just a minute and you can go get another one."

About those pliers: In ground-fishing days, every boat had a pair of those pliers handy for removing fishhooks that by accident snagged a fisherman in the thumb or the back of his neck, and perhaps in a more vital place. The skipper, who would be the ranking medical office aboard, quickly jerked the hook so the barb showed on the other side of the flesh, cut the barbed end away with the pliers' cutter, and then backed the unbarbed wire from the wound. It was done deftly in a twinkling, and a disinfectant poured on. Mrs. Thomas had no barb to cut off, but the pliers gave her a good grip on my splinter, and I thought I'd been struck by lightning. It bled, but she was ready, and that's what they do out there if something happens.

Mrs. Thomas put on a J&J, and told Han to keep an eye on me and watch for infection. That's really how Han and I came to get acquainted but it didn't really ease my mother and Mrs. Crowthers when they worried.

Han dried the pliers well, rubbed them with machine oil, and put them back on the sloop.

Chapter 11

MY BATHING SUIT

Going ahead and going back, as I try to sort out the sequence of our Morning River adventures, bewilders me, and as I try to bring this particular part into focus, I'd guess it was a bit over ten years ago (I'm in Philadelphia today and it is winter) that my mother looked up from her water-color box to say, "What about swimming?" The previous summer my father had either bought or was planning to buy Morning River Farm, and I'm sure my mother had not yet accepted that she would become a Maine summer resident, although sociably she was ready and took pleasure at the thought of being in the *Bulletin* every time she went to or came from her "seasonable property." My father, having yet to write a check for Morning River, hadn't indulged himself that way, and had only acquired some huge travel-trunks and a half dozen suitcases. We'd need to take some things along.

My father mentioned this one day in the Pennsy Railroad offices, asking the best place to buy such, and one of the railroad executives had said, "Go over to the maintenance offices and find Joe-joe Clark." "Them as has, gits," runs the old saw, and Joe-joe Clark was in charge of unclaimed baggage. The next morning but one a truck came to our house, leaving four enormous "steamer" trunks and the suitcases. All had been in the Pennsy warehouse for several years, long enough for claiming to elapse, and now my father owned them as well as their unstipulated contents. Only one, I found, had anything in it of possible use, and I counted out twenty-three wooden coat hangers from the Parker House in Boston. They went to Maine the next summer, and are still in the closets at Morning River Farm.

The steamer trunk of those days had just about the capacity of a hall closet in a house. It was rectangular except for the top, which was hinged and rounded. The round top was to keep railroad and steamboat baggagemen from putting one on top of another and crushing the bottom one. But baggagemen simply stood these trunks on end and piled them high with rounded covers on one side. These that came to our house had not been crushed and were in perfect shape. Each had drawers and shelves, and it took a great deal of personal belongings to fill one. My mother started right in, and was ready to go to Maine long before my father inquired about routes and tickets. And tucked away in some spot or another were my two bathing suits. Along with everything else from dish wipers and window curtains to my father's white linen golf knickers and the American flag.

I could swim at eight, and well enough to have a safety certificate. I took lessons at the pool in my father's club, and I don't remember if I got to be a lawful lifeguard and could rescue shipwrecked sailors, but I had passed tests. Not always, but at certain times I had to wear a swimsuit in the club pool, and my mother thought I should have a new outfit for Maine. When she had asked, "What about swimming?" my father had said the ocean was available year round, but Morning River froze up from July to June.

And it turned out that as our trunks and suitcases were emptied at Morning River and things laid away and hung up for our first summer, the bathing suits and the swim trunks my mother had bought for me were put away, and I didn't just know where. We'd have to find them.

The Elzada flip hour was to be reinstated later, so none was held that first afternoon, and Mrs. Thomas said she had clam cakes on the make and everybody would have them and lobsters for supper at her house—the Marcoux house. Mrs. Crowthers could help her if she wished, but Mrs. Crowthers needn't give a thought to making supper up at the big house. And by this time it was afternoon and we were settled in. Han had led me across to the old mill and the boat shop, and I began seeing the things belonging to Morning River Farm, starting with the sawmill and the big water wheel in the spillway under what was to become our Croze Nest, but was now the shop where Jabez Knight and Jules Marcoux made barrels and tubs. The bucket shop.

This was my first moment alone with Han, and in my recollection she was easy to be with. Her smile would never make her anything but friends, and the tinkly laugh that came with it was beautiful. Her yellow hair, loose and "all up and down the mast" was orderly if seemingly uncombed and unarranged, and I'll just say she was fun to be with and I realized already that she and I would be mostly together. She led me out the catwalk so we stood at the edge of the considerable pool where the mill spillway goes into the salt-water estuary of Morning River, where tidewater begins.

"Swim?" says Han.

"Yes," I said, and then, imitating the Thomas family, I spoke my first word in Yankee. "Eyah," I added.

Han said, "Good!" and kicked off her sneakers, threw off her shirt and pants, and dove into the spillway pool.

It was as sudden as that. She kicked herself about and came back, climbing to the ramp beside me, and she said, "C'mon in!"

We did the talking later. I dropped my clothes, jumped in, and Han and I stayed in the pool quite some time. When we did talk, I told her my swim togs were at the house, but I wasn't sure where, and Han told me she didn't own a bathing suit. She said out at Monhegan Island, where she went swimming alone, the water was freezy cold all summer and she didn't like it. So

she didn't need a suit much anyway. In here, when she was looking around before the Thomases came to Morning River, she'd
found this pool below the mill, and the water was a great deal
warmer than anything out around the island, even the pond there.
The estuary warmed it up. She'd been in several times before I
came. Han said, "I don't think I need a bathing suit."

She had a towel, and we dried each other. Her hair dried
and she knotted a string around it. "A piece of ganging," she
said, to rhyme with changing, which is a down-Maine word for
some fishline. When the time came we put our clothes on and
went over for clam cakes. Nobody asked if we'd been swimming. I believe that in so many words nobody ever asked, but
at the same time everybody knew. And my mother always knew
that my swim suit never left the hook in my bedroom closet. And
Mr. and Mrs. Thomas knew that Han didn't have any.

There were summer afternoons unsuited for a swim, but
not too many each year, and Han and I didn't skip too often.
We did, and also not too often, swim at other places, such as at
Manny's Cove on Razor Island, and at the bend in the river in
our trout "rain barrel," but never where we'd be seen.

We simply never thought anything about it, or felt there
was reason to. And it may well be that our folks felt, after a
few summers, that it was too late to question something that began properly enough in childhood innocence. Han and I didn't
give the matter a thought.

47

Chapter 12

HADDOCK CHOWDER

Lacking any conveniences, we really "roughed it" at Morning River Farm during our early summers. My father quickly gave up the idea of a windmill for a generator, and ordered an alternating current job with diesel power, but everything had to wait until the houses were wired and we got appliances. A man came from Portland by boat to wire the houses. We did have two big ice chests, but nobody had cut ice for them since the days of Jabez and Jules. In older days ice was cut every January and stored in the ice house under sawdust from the mill. Mr. Thomas was planning to have ice cut that next winter, but on our first summer we had no refrigeration. So one morning Mr. Thomas had an errand on the island, and on the way back he dallied briefly at the right spot and brought back a haddock. Han and I ran to the wharf to be there when he touched, and he sent us to the Marcoux house with the haddock so "Marm" could get the fire to it before the day's heat did. Start the thing cooking! Mrs. Thomas was glad to have a haddock and sent Han up to the other house so Mrs. Crowthers could come down and see how to make a chowder. Mrs. Crowthers, I think you've heard, didn't believe in fish.

Han's mother told Mrs. Crowthers that in the long run

you can't beat haddock chowder. When Han got back, she was sent to the cellar to get salt pork from the brine barrel, and the haddock was filleted and chunked before she came up with the pork. "Now!" said Mrs. Thomas.

Among the cooking pots inherited from Marie-Paule Marcoux herself was a great cast iron pot with a cover, and it was already heating on the stove when the chunk (junk said Mrs. Thomas) of salt pork was sliced and diced and ready to go in. The pork sizzled when dropped in, and Mrs. Thomas kept moving it about with a flipper. Then Han took over, and right away she said, "Ready here!" Mrs. Thomas dumped in the cut-up onions and the diced potatoes and covered them with water; they need longer cooking than the haddock. Mrs. Crowthers wasn't missing a single move, but feigned disinterest as she protested that no art could make any fish fit to eat. Mrs. Crowthers said, "I suppose the onions help kill the fishy taste?"

Mrs. Thomas did look as if she had a sly word about folks from Philadelphia, but she didn't offer it. She said, "Some." Then she explained, "We don't see too much fresh milk here, so we use either canned milk or dry milk and make do. I use dry milk, and then add Carnation to give it body. No substitute is ever 'just as good' but we make out. And always heat the milk so it won't curdle." The haddock meat and the milk were added after I left.

Han and I didn't wait around, but Mrs. Crowthers did, and she was late coming up to our house to make dinner. During dinner she told my mother every last secret about making a true Maine chowder, and admitted freely that it was by no means a complicated dish and that it was barely possible it might be fit to eat.

But the haddock chowder wasn't for tonight, Mrs. Crowthers said. It had to "mull,' so it wouldn't be ready until tomorrow. "Tomorrow I get the night off and we all eat at the other house," she said, and in spite of her dislike for fish, I thought she sounded as if she were looking forward to it.

But there was one thing Mrs. Thomas didn't tell Mrs.

Crowthers about during that cooking lesson. When Han and I left, and Mrs. Thomas was still putting the haddock chowder together, Han took a pail and a clam hoe, and we went down to the gut and dug about a quart of clams. These, Mrs. Thomas steamed off, and she saved the water. Han and I and Mrs. Thomas ate the clams that afternoon and nobody missed them, but Mrs. Thomas poured about a pint of the clam juice into the haddock chowder, while it was mulling.

That haddock chowder kept on mulling that afternoon, and cooled down when the fire dwindled during the night. It warmed again and mulled again all the second day. At supper time we assembled at the Marcoux house, seven of us, and the chowder was decanted into the very bowl Marie-Paule Marcoux had used for haddock chowders all her life. Mrs. Crowthers pronounced the chowder elegant. There were no dissenters.

Mrs. Thomas was plainly pleased to have approval from a Philadelphia cook, and said, "I didn't make a big thing of the clam juice. Always add clam juice. Any fish perks up with a cup of clam juice. Fish chowder, clam chowder, lobster stew, oyster stew, shrimp and scallops. I didn't tell you because it's a secret."

Chapter 13

NOW
CUNNERS

That evening at table, after we Philadelphians had praised the down-Maine haddock chowder (with Mrs. Crowthers graciously concurring!), Mrs. Thomas said, "All right. But I'll be honest with you! Take a week or so to get haddock off your minds, and I'll make you a far better fish chowder! Right, Han?" Han said just one word: "Cunners?"

Mr. Thomas took this as a cue. He said, "I'll have to fix a new cunner line; my hook's rusted bad." Han pointed at me and said, "Two!"

Mr. Thomas said, "Right, two." So Han took me fishing for cunners, and Mrs. Thomas made a cunner chowder.

The dictionary says the cunner is a small fish common to the North Atlantic Coast. Han told me it is some kind of an ocean perch, hard as the devil to skin, and the sweetest chowder fish of them all. She said we'd need "nigh" a pailful for one of her mother's chowders, and that called for a lot of skinning. Mr. Thomas did make up two new cunner lines; each of about two fathoms of light twine with a trout hook and a shingle nail for a sinker. No rod—the line was wound on a short pine stick.

Just about two weeks, and Mrs. Thomas asked us to find her enough cunners. Han said we'd have some wading to do, and we had our two new cunner lines in a pail. The tide had just turned and was beginning to come in when we set out. We crossed Morning River on the mill dam and walked down the shore about a quarter of a mile. Here, a ledge made out and it flattened on the seaward end so we had a place to stand. Han made me study the ledge on the way out, because in places it would be under water when we came back. "Cunners bite on the coming tide," she said.

Having no idea what a cunner would look like, I waited to be shown. Han unwound some of the cunner lines, and then took a piece of paper from her shirt pocket. "Need bait for just the first one," she said, "and if you don't get a first one you go home. Some days they've all gone to church." She put a small cube of salt pork on the hook and handed me the pine stick. The tide was already climbing the face of the ledge. Han was putting some pork on the second hook. "Feel the nail on the bottom and lift two feet," she said. "And cunners don't bite hard. You may not know it's a bite. You gotta jerk to hook one."

Han had a cunner at once. She cut that one to get bait for another and immediately had a second cunner. "You gotta jerk," she repeated. The cunner is a small fish. Nothing like that chowder haddock. Then I had one, and Han said, "Don't stick the fins in your hand! They can squirm and stab you! Hold them close to the gills and drop them in the pail. Be careful! Get stuck, and it may poison you some."

Then Han said we were getting some good-sized cunners. Bigger than last time. The tide was running now and taking our lines with it, so we were getting cunners and usually two at once. Han said we had all we'd need for a chowder, and we could come off the ledge before the tide covered it. We came off, but Han wouldn't let me carry the pail of fish. "Cunners stop at high water," she said, "and if you spill these—no chowder!"

When we got back to our wharf in the estuary, Han showed me a spike driven into a spile and said, "Here's our hang-up!" I was about to be instructed in the art of making cunners ready for the pot! The cunner, as Han had indicated, is spiny, and his fins can wound. He is accordingly difficult to skin, and he needs to be skinned before his small fillet of pure white meat is cut away from the backbone with a sharp knife. Mr. Thomas had whet two knives for us, and Han showed me how to use the spike in the spile. Belly towards, the cunner is put to the spike, mouth and gill, and small cuts made for a place to start the skin. With a thumb pressing hard on the blade of his knife, the skinner peels the skin away, revealing the meat. Han said, "Nothing to it if you know how!" And after a couple of cunners, Han said I knew how. "The rest is just one after another," she said.

Mr. Thomas came with a broom and a pail about the time we had our dressed cunners in our pail, and he said, "How'll you swap?" He took the cleaned fish and I began sloshing water on the wharf and sweeping our gurry into the estuary. "That's what makes fat eels," said Han. "They say they wait under the wharf for somebody to skin cunners. You skin an eel the same way, off that same spike, but I never have and don't plan to this afternoon."

I told Han I'd never seen an eel.

She said, "They're not beautiful."

Mrs. Thomas said we had more than enough cunners, and her chowder would be underway immediately, if not sooner. Not tonight, but tomorrow night. She said she'd need another small snatch of clams. "Get small ones," she said, "steamers. And maybe Mrs. Crowthers would like to help again?"

In my opinion, without waiting for that of Mrs. Crowthers, a cunner chowder is superior to that of a haddock chowder, but if you can get a haddock it spares you the tricky job of skinning cunners. Even though Han says, "It's easy if you know how."

A postscript about cunners for summercaters and folks from away: Cunners like a rocky bottom, rather than sandy beaches and mud flats. Where humanity has intruded, they no longer come to some shores, but they are still taken off some wharves and piers, and off ledges. Periwinkles make suitable bait; crush the winkle shell with a rock, and fix the muscle part to your hook. Use the coming tide. A good place is off the end of the long breakwater in Rockland Harbor. No rod is necessary, but a small telescope rod from a sporting shop can lend dignity to otherwise workaday angling. Han always spit on her bait for luck, a superstitions attributed to The Banks. Clam juice, to be added to your chowder for superb flavor, may be had in the supermarkets, gourmet shelf, under bouillon.

Chapter 14

PAYING TAXES TO THE STATE

So at a flip hour one evening Mr. Thomas got around to explaining why my father paid his taxes in Augusta, and along with flip and taxes and Elzada, and other things, my father strengthened his interest in the history of Morning River and what he could do to keep the place from changing. Mr. Thomas said Maine had always had a great deal of wild land and where there was no local government the state was in charge. When an uninhabited place got enough people, it could petition the state legislature and become a plantation, a town, or a city, assess taxes, have its schools, build its roads, and have a name. Monhegan Island, he said, had lately decided to become a plantation, which was a name used in earliest times, and now the people on Monhegan paid their taxes at home. The time might come, he supposed, when Morning River would have enough people to do that, and my father said, "Over my dead body!" That's what ticked my father off and made him very purposeful about keeping folks from away just as far away as he could. He began buying pieces of land to make a buffer zone around this Morning River property with everything in trust forever.

Which gave my father something to do! Until now, he had one solid and permanent rule about Morning River—he was not to be disturbed by anything while he was on his Maine vacation. He wasn't going to do anything while he was here except to sit around.

Then one afternoon Mr. Thomas said there was a deed from a king of France for Morning River Farm, as well as an English deed. My father said, "I've seen it! Land was conveyed by a governor in Nova Scotia, and the deed is recorded in York County."

So this was something my father knew about that Mr. Thomas hadn't heard. The English deed, which Jabez Knight had in the beginning, gave the land only to the high tide mark. Below the average high tide, the land went with the ocean and belonged to the people. But the French deed, which my father had found when looking up the title before he bought Morning River, conveyed our land to the low tide mark. My father said, "I'm sure it was custom, but I didn't find another low-tide deed on record. Maybe we're the only one."

Mr. Thomas said the acreage of the Morning River Farm was smaller than a customary Maine township, so my father made a hand-sketched map that included our land somewhere in the middle, but as much again around about. This was the "township" he hoped some day to own, and which would be kept forever as "uninhabited." Nobody from away would ever come here to live.

It was that same morning of the flip hour revival that my father came down to breakfast to say, "I'm going to Boston." My mother never asked the why of any of his few trips, and now he added, "It's got to be Boston."

My mother said, "Yes?"

"About those French tidewater deeds! I suppose they're good, but I don't know that they are. I don't think we need to go to some archive in Canada. Boston, probably. I'm going to step down and ask Sherm if he's free."

So my father got the afternoon train to Boston, and was gone three days. He came back by boat to Rockland, got a ride to Port Clyde, and Cousin Snood brought him to Morning River in time for the flip hour. Cousin Snood spent the night. My father was full of joy. He'd found just what he wanted, and what he had expected to find.

"Poor old fellow sitting there," he told all of us and Mr. Thomas, "and I guess nobody had spoken to him since the big Tea Party. He was lonesome. Delighted to have me call. What could he do for me? Well, he had it all. The deed to Morning River from King Louis the fourteenth to one Cadillac, dated 1603, is good as wheat, because Maine was then New France. Then, when Canada became English, all those deeds were confirmed, and again in 1787 those in Maine were confirmed again by Massachusetts. Then when Maine became a state in 1820, Maine agreed to all such deeds previously confirmed by Massachusetts. And one more thing: in 1820, when Maine became one of the United States, Congress required Maine to agree to everything Massachusetts had done, including our little strip of tidewater. I don't know how much, but it's between three and four acres anyway. The little man hidden away in the Boston state house showed me everything, and you want to know? Our Jabez Knight didn't just build boats. He was smart with his law, and every paper in the pile was in order and correct. That would be Elzada's father, the very first flipper at Morning River!

My father told my mother, "This is just starting. When I get through we'll have Morning River set apart so no strangers can come here and organize and tell us what to do!"

Chapter 15

OUR
LANCH

After the *America*'s convincing victory, Queen Victoria was told, "Second, Your Majesty? There is no second!" So it was with the lanch of our sailing dory. No other happening at Morning River Farm equaled that lanch as an introduction to Maine and to Maine people. Han's mother and father, and Han, had come in from Monhegan Island to get our place ready for our first arrival from Philadelphia, and Han had gone through all the buildings to look things over. Far up on the beams of the sawmill roof she had found a boat, tucked away in a manner probably meant to be permanent. Her father had climbed up to look, and surmised it was the sailing dory Jabez Knight had built as a boy back at Bristol in sixteen-hundred-and-something—the dory he had sailed down east to Morning River when he first came. It had been carefully fitted into its space under the roof so it would take some work and some ingenuity to get it out and again into the water. It was in perfect condition, and since Jabez Knight was well storied as a master craftsman the carpentry indicated the boat was his work. That sailing dory was one of the first things Han showed me after we got acquainted and knew we were to share growing-up at Morning River Farm. And not long afterwards Mr. Thomas told us the boat could be brought down all right, and "perhaps" some day we'd have a lanch and get to use the boat.

Although Jabez Knight and Jules Marcoux had built many boats at Morning River, this was the only boat that came with the property; otherwise, there was the lobster-fishing sloop of Mr. Thomas, which belonged on Monhegan Island.

That dory consumed Han and me. We'd stand so we could look up at it and dream of the voyages we'd make. It also consumed attention from Mr. Thomas, who meditated constantly on how the devil Jabez and Jules got her up there in the first place, and how he was about to get her down. He figured the sawmill had been completed before it was decided to put the boat up on the beams. Accordingly certain beams were removed to get the dory into place, and then replaced, hemming her in. The same beams would have to be removed again to get her out. The dory was just shy of twenty feet, Mr. Thomas said, but dories are substantial boats and a twenty-foot is a fairly heavy craft. Something besides manpower had been necessary, and Mr. Thomas said he had heard that Jules Marcoux had gone to Nova Scotia with his sloop and brought home a yoke of oxen. Mr. Thomas laughed at the thought.

He said cattle are very poor sailors, and the experience Jules had sailing his oxen home was certainly one of a kind. On leaving Port Royal Jules had hit an unfortunate southeast wind that, combined with the usual cross-chop of a Fundy tide, had brought his cattle to their knees in front, leaving their after anatomy aloft, and for two days they had blatted without cease and defecated without shame. Unloading the steers at the Morning River wharf with the derrick and a sling was an unpleasant job, and it took two days to clean the sloop. Then it took three days to clean Jules. So Mr. Thomas presumed that the sailing dory had been moved up onto the beams with pulleys and ropes, and a pair of oxen.

Mr. Thomas told Han and me that mechanics had been well understood by the ancient people. "They built the pyramids, didn't they?" The screw, the lever, the wedge, no great mystery—but what did Jabez and Jules use for a purchase? I asked Han what a purchase might be, and she said it was something to tie to, a place to stand.

Then one afternoon Mr. Thomas stood up—he'd been sitting on a lobster crate—and he said, "I've got it! Only answer! Has to be!" He walked around the sawmill and up the riverbank about fifty yards. There was an outcropping of ledge there, not more than eight inches above the river level. And he found his "purchase."

"We can have our lanch a week from next Sunday," he said. What he'd found was a hole drilled in the ledge, now full of dirt and he began to dig it out with a screwdriver. "They put an eyebolt in there, and I suppose the ice took the bolt out long ago," he said. "We'll put it back again!"

My father was afraid of boats, but told Mr. Thomas to do whatever he wished. And he said under no circumstances were the youngsters to be allowed alone in the dory until they knew how to handle her and themselves. Mr. Thomas said he'd need some help, and would get his cousins Manfred and Snood, and Snood knew a man with a quarry horse from Gotts Island. The horse was blind, so would ride in a boat all right.

Mr. Thomas took his sloop to the mainland to get some timbers and planks he'd need for a lanching runway and a platform, and swung around on the way back to alert Manfred and Snood. They came two days later.

Han and I were impatient. This was to be our boat, and summer after summer we used it. We never went any great distance in it, and we never got into any trouble. It was certainly an antique and an oddity, and if we went beyond Razor Island Gut we were sure to encounter a fishing boat to admire us, and sometimes pleasure boats with people who looked at us through binoculars.

Manfred and Snood were precious. Manfred was a good seven feet tall, and Snood was barely five feet. Brothers? Mr. Thomas explained that their mother had been the lighthouse keeper and her light was always on. But when Mr. Thomas showed them the stored dory they knew what needed to be done and went right at it. That was when I learned that a lanch, down Maine way, is never lightly approached and requires exuberance, enthusiasm, and complete coordination.

The next fall, after I was back in school at Philadelphia, I told my teacher about the lanch we had at Morning River Farm. Now, truthfully, our dory had had its lanch back when she was built by Jabez Knight, and we didn't know anything about that. We were merely putting her back in the water after she'd been hauled and stored. A boat gets lanched once. But it had been quite a few years since a real lanch had been held in the Monhegan region and everybody was willing to stretch the definitions for the sake of the exercises. Manfred and Snood weren't about to nit-pick.

So when I told my school teacher in Philadelphia that we had held a lanch, she really didn't know one lanch from another, but she did tell me the word is pronounced lawnch. I told her I'd heard them say lanch, and she shamed me in front of the others and made me stand up and say lawnch. For the first and only time in my life I said lawnch. I told my father about that, and he said, "An A student never disputes his teacher."

But even if this wasn't a true lanch, we made it do. Cousin Snood said the dory should have a name, and after Han decided "dory" would be the right name he climbed up with a paint brush and neatly brushed DORY on the stern. Cousin Snood suggested Mrs. Crowthers for sponsor and took a few moments to show her how to swing the bottle and cry out, "I name thee DORY!" Mr. Thomas had found an eyebolt for the hole in the ledge, and had rigged his pulleys and rope. A lobsterman was bringing the horse in his power boat, and bringing food was delegated to another lobsterman. The lobster smack was bringing the lobster buyer from Portland, a bottle of wine for Mrs. Crowthers to swing, and improbably a photographer from the *Philadelphia Bulletin*, and we never did find out how the *Bulletin* knew.

My mother and Mrs. Crowthers had no idea how to prepare food for a lanch, but Mrs. Thomas did, and she superintended that, and there were some comical moments as Mrs. Crowthers was instructed. My father, who was not greatly excited about staging an authentic lanch, told Mrs. Thomas to "go all out," and he gave her a blank check for the lobsterman to take to the store in Port Clyde. As a consequence, Mrs. Thomas kept telling Mrs. Crowthers "not to stint," until Mrs. Crowthers asked what stint meant in Monhegan.

The lanch was held on a Sunday, and Mr. Thomas had tried to get the mission boat *Sunbeam* to come to lend dignity, but the skipper pleaded a prior engagement at the Loud's Island pulpit. Cousin Snood volunteered that the minister didn't care to risk being seen at a lanch on Sunday where un-Christian revelry might occur. Cousin Snood added, "Like me!", so the minister was probably justified.

The lobster smack brought the bottle of rum Mr. Thomas had suggested my father provide, and also two bottles as a gift from the lobster buyer, and also a bottle from the Harris brothers, a ship chandlery at Portland Harbor.

My father knew nothing about lanches, and said to Cousin Snood that he had not expected to see the rum, as he had been told that Maine was a prohibition state. Cousin Snood assured him the rum was strictly for mechanical and medicinal purposes and was to be used only at the discretion of the lanch master, should any of the lanching crew be so unfortunate as to pinch his finger with the dog shore. Cousin Snood said at polite lanches nobody was allowed above five pinches with the dog shore. The Pilgrim fathers, Cousin Snood said, always lanched on water alone, and adding some rum was a Maine improvement on the grounds that Pilgrim lanches were never all that much fun. Cousin Snood said the dog shore was the wedge that held the boat back until everybody got a pinched finger. Just then Mrs. Crowthers cried out in pain.

All was ready well before the hour of the lanch, which was at high tide. The moon was full that evening. The dory would not slide down greased ways, as larger vessels do, but would be pulled all the way by the horse and the rope. Mrs. Crowthers, with bouquet and bottle, was at the right place and ready, practicing her swing and saying, "I name thee Dory!" Manfred led off the horse, and the dory smoothly came off the beams and moved over the platform to the ramp. Now the horse was stopped, and Han and I were ceremoniously handed into the dory. Custom calls for the owner to be lanched aboard, and this was to be our craft. The horse was led on.

Making no splash, and without a ripple, our dory went stern-first into the estuary, and Mrs. Crowthers cried, "I name thee Dory!" and swung her bottle. She missed, and her momentum carried her overboard. Cousin Snood had seemingly foreseen this possibility, and retrieved her neatly, as she clutched her bouquet to her bosom and allowed Cousin Snood to take the unscathed bottle. Han and I were afloat.

We hand-paddled the dory to the wharf and made it secure, and then we sat on the sternsheets and held hands. Mrs. Thomas saved us more than we could eat, but we missed the banquet. The Coast Guard boys came ashore, and they sang some songs, and Han and I heard that from where we sat. Later on Cousin Snood walked Mrs. Crowthers over to the wharf, and she broke the wine bottle on our dory's prow.

Since everybody from Monhegan Island had been to our lanch, we had been fully introduced to all our neighbors. My father would say to Mr. Thomas, "Now, just who are Herb and Irene?" He remembered their first names. Mr. Thomas would say, "He lobsters." And then, sometimes weeks later, he'd say to my father, "Saw Herb today. He was asking about the dory." That was good. It sort of took the edge off being from Philadelphia.

Chapter 16

SCULLING

When we had the big lanch for the antique sailing dory of Jabez Knight, Cousin Snood promised to come some time and show Han and me how to scull. Then he didn't come, and we supposed he'd forgotten all about it, and about three summers later he showed up right after noontime and wanted to know if we were ready for the sculling lesson. He said, "It did take me a few minutes to get things ready." As far as we ever knew, getting ready meant a sculling oar, of which he made two, so we had a spare, and a board with a hole in it through which the sculling oar was handled. I knew not one thing about sculling, but Han said her father could scull and had a skiff with a sculling port. It's a way to row a small boat by twisting a sculling oar back and forth at the stern. Cousin Snood said it could be mighty useful in a dory in an emergency, and a lot easier than working sweeps. Han told me what all that meant.

One of the boats often used in Maine that call for sculling is a gunning float, used for ducks and geese. The sculling oar is not seen and makes no commotion, so the hunter can get close to a raft of birds. Cousin Snood said if we lost a breeze, we'd be glad to know how to scull our dory. With that he said he'd be back soon, and sure enough—here he was two Augusts

64

later. It was August, all right, because we'd had thick-o'-fog for a week and Mrs. Crowthers couldn't get her bureau drawers open. The fog hung in, and there was no breath for our spritsail. Cousin Snood fastened his hole in the board at the stern with two joiner's clamps, ran his oar through, and said, "Cast off!" I cast, and we three pushed and jumped in.

Han had seen her father scull, but to me the whole thing was brand new, and somewhat comical. Cousin Snood sat there on the sternsheets, one hand to the oar, which he had made and given a special shape, and just wiggled his hand. Any dory is heavy, so sculling is not the usual way to make one go. But shortly the oar began to do its work and our dory made headway. Next we were going right along. We didn't go far, since this was for practice, so Cousin Snood changed places and I worked the oar. Next, Han. Cousin Snood knelt handy by and told us how to work the oar. We went back and forth several times, and at last fetched up the wharf. Cousin Snood said, "You may never need to scull, but you know how. Shall we look into the flip situation?"

Han and I didn't try for our usual swim that afternoon, but went to the Marcoux house with Cousin Snood, where we enjoyed his tale about the time he tangled with the YEWnited States Navy "on the Lord's Holy Sabbath in just such a fogmull as we been having this week."

This was the first time I'd heard this tale, but Han whispered that she grew up on it. She also said the story was true, except for Cousin Snood's literary additions.

"Just such a fogmull," he began, "and it hung on and on closer than the bark to a tree, and they warn't a man on the Coast of Maine had been beyond his bait house for a week. And now it was Sunday, and I was determined I warn't going to let a fuss o' fog deprive me of the comfort and solace I get from my Sunday meeting. So I wrapped my Bible in some sailcloth, and found a fifty cent piece for the collection, and I just twisted the bilge-wheel on my sainted Smith & Langmaid, and I strikes out for T'Hahb'h for divine worship, relying on our heavenly father to bring me in through a fog worse than any feather tick. And I guess I missed that second left hand turn, because all at once I sensed that Tents Hahb'h had gone and got moved, and I didn't know where I was except I warn't anywhere near it. I hate to admit it, but I was lost. Now, to make matters worse, this was war time, and Old Kaiser Bill had his U-boats over here making trouble, and most of our coast was closed off to us. How did I know I warn't over the line? Not only that, but some of the closed off water was mined. At least we were told so. If I was over the line, they'd take my boat and talk to me in coarse language and all that.

"Well, I couldn't see anything, so I listened in the fog, and I didn't hear a thing that gave me any kind of fix, so I decided the thing to do was to toss the killick and stay put. I had my Bible so I could improvise my own Sunday-go-to-meeting. It was warm and if the fog should scale off it would be a scorcher. And that's just what I did.

"I had God all to myself there in that burgoo fog, and I do say if He was small on navigation, He was big on Salvation, because He made first-rate company and we had a bang-up good meeting. Then I was pondering some passage in Revelations, and my thoughts were disturbed by an odd noise that was hardly tuned to Gospel. It came and went, but it didn't seem to come from one place or another. But it did give me an echo, and right away I figured out where I was.

"Instead of being over in the Georges River, as I surmised I was, I was right up in here—back of Big Razor Island, in Razor Island Gut, and if I could-a seen anything, I'd-a been looking right square at this house, here. I was sure some old flap-doodled at that! Then I decided this noise I kept hearing was a boat engine. Had to be. It sure warn't a one-lunger like I had, or anybody else in those days, but it had to be a real fine marine job. Then, I would hear this little whirrr of an engine, and then a ding-ding-ding like a bell. Yes, I did. I thought I'd got the ding-dings. Whirrr-whirrr-ding-ding! I couldn't concentrate on my Bible lesson worth a cent. Fact is, I was finally sitting there looking off into the fog, soft as a custard. But just then there come a wisp of air and enough fog scaled off so I could see, and what do you know? There was a boat!

"That's what I'd been hearing. I just got one click at her and she was gone into the fog, but that whirrr noise was her engine, and she was one pretty piece of boat. Yewnited States Navy boat. Out of my sight, the thing went ding-ding-ding on a bell, the whirrr stopped, and here she came backing up so I thought she was going to ram me. Then she ding-dinged again, and went full speed forward and stopped dead. Somebody had seen me. Close up like that I could see what she was. She was one of those torpedo-boat destroyers they had around 1917 and 1918, and I'd seen a couple of them over at Boothbay Harbor. Beautiful craft, away over-powered, and smooth as a schoolmarm's leg. Each one ten times worth what it cost to make ten. There was a sailor in the wheelhouse, and he was the one kept dingling the bell. He was a good jingler, as he brought the limousine to a halt right by the hitching post. Another sailor showed up, and he grabbed my coaming with a garft that had a pink tea cosy on the hook. Lah-de-dah!

"Well, next came the admiral. Out of a companionway. He was in full uniform, and he had Burpee's Seed Catalog up and down his front, so he looked like the salad bar at Charlie Miller's restaurant in Bangor, and by the Lord Harry, what do you know, he salutes me!

"Fact! I clutches my Bible just before it hits the flooring, very awkward in such high-class company, and he says, 'And who are you?' Now, putting two and two together, I had decided our Yewnited States Navy was gone to hell, so I wasn't rightly in dignified respect and under the circumstances I didn't feel it was the admiral's privilege to ask me who I was. I didn't know why that foolish boat was cruising up and down behind Big Razor Island in a thick-o'-fog, but it seemed to me that was the case, and who I was didn't really make much matter. So I says, standing in a respectful posture, 'My compliments, sir, but I ain't lost. May I ask, instead, if I can help you?'

"So another admiral comes topside, and I guess he sees there's something in this, and he says, 'Tooshay! Tell me, Captain, just where the hell we are?'

"That was some better. So I says, 'Certainly. My pleasure! You're four fathoms west of Big Razor Island in Razor Island Gut.'

"He says, 'Yes.' Then he stepped closer to me and winked so I knew he was going to be on my side, and he says, 'Before we go any farther, may I ask how you happened to be out here this morning?'

"I said, 'Glad you asked! I'm out here on God's business, and you have interrupted my Sabbath devotions. I was pondering the sixth chapter of Revelations, verse one, when I heard your dingle-ding.' I stood up, holding my Bible so he could see it, and he nodded first, and then shook his head, and he said to the admiral, 'If-you-please-sir.' 'Your hail?' he said to me.

" 'Monhegan Island.'

" 'Is that near?'

" 'About ten tubs of trawl.'

" 'Now, cut that out! I was born in Jonesport. Give us a fix for Boothbay Harbor.'

" 'Morning River Farm dead ahead. Due west, and second turn to the right. Look for Red Turner's white horse by the schoolhouse.'

" 'That's more like it,' he says.

"So I suggested they wait out the fog, assuming they had food, and I guess that's what they done. They had a crew of six, and were doing trials with this new boat, and decided to look at the Sheepscott River, and got lost when the fog shut in. They'd been going back and forth all that morning in Razor Island Gut and couldn't find out how to get out of it. They'd go a ways, tinkle the bell, and go the other way. They honked me, and I left them anchored right off the sawmill. I made it to the island all right. I did wonder some if that white horse in Revelations said anything to the Yewnited States Navy when they come to Ned Turner's and the schoolhouse.

"Thanks for the lunch!"

Once again, Cousin Snood was on his way to the island.

Chapter 17

THE HAKE
DAY

Mrs. Crowthers hadn't gone downstairs to the kitchen yet, so it was well before breakfast time. A beautiful June morning; soon after our arrival from Philadelphia. Mr. Thomas was not a man to take charge and give orders in a loud voice, so we paid attention when we heard him shout. He called, "Up and out, everybody, there's work to do!" Upstairs, we heard him all right, though he wasn't inside our house. He'd opened the back door enough to stick his head in.

I was downstairs first, and then Mrs. Crowthers, and my mother and father right behind. Mr. Thomas was now in the kitchen, and he said, "Beach is covered with silver hake! A sight to see!"

Han and Mrs. Thomas were already on the beach, down where our estuary runs into the gut, and even from our distance, not far, we could see shining silver that would be hake when we got closer.

Later on, after the excitement, Mr. Thomas explained. In bygone years it was usual about every year to have schools of silver hake appear along the coast, and there were several explanations of why they ran up onto the shore and stranded themselves. Some said dogfish drove them. Others felt moonlight attracted them, but then they'd appear on moonless nights. Whatever it was, millions of beautiful silvery fish, such as we had now found all along our shore, would be waiting in the morning. Hake, Mr. Thomas said, is an excellent food fish, and as the morning was cool he thought he could run some over to Tenants Harbor or Port Clyde before they spoiled, and he'd stop at the bank on his way home. Han and Mrs. Thomas were already filling baskets and clam hods with hake.

That WAS a sight to see. All along the high-tide line on our side of the gut the fish were laid orderly. Mr. Thomas said this was the largest cast-up in many years, and in some recent years there hadn't been any show of hake at all. Too bad, as Maine people like hake and a very good day's pay was right there to be picked up. Get them to town and they'd go like hotcakes. By now Mr. Thomas was carrying the baskets to dump the fish in his sloop, and the rest of us were helping Han and her mother to pick up fish. Mr. Thomas rigged a tarpaulin over the fish in the sloop and called, "Gulls'll find these any minute now, and we'll have a fight on our hands!" But the gulls held off until he had enough to take to market. Then he said to Han, "If I run these over, do you want to corn what you can? Plenty of salt in the old baithouse. I'll be back before too long."

Mr. Thomas had scarcely cleared the estuary when the seagulls arrived. And they didn't come one and then another. They scaled in with great cry and settled down by the hundreds. Where had they been, and what brought the news? They had no fear of people, and their wings almost, but didn't, brush us as they lighted on the windrow of fish. We got several baskets of hake to the wharf, and had them covered with sailcloth and boards before Han said, "That's enough!" The screaming gulls made so much noise we had to leave the beach.

I think my mother and father didn't join in the corned hake processing wholeheartedly, but Han quickly showed me how to open a hake for salting, and Mrs. Thomas had good luck convincing Mrs. Crowthers a corned hake was worth going after.

It did turn out to be easier than I expected. Using the same salt Mr. Thomas bought in bags for keeping his lobster bait, we rubbed it generously on an opened hake, and then we rubbed some more on another hake. Salted, the fish meat was cured, and would keep for a long time. Mrs. Thomas gave Mrs. Crowthers the full lecture on the many uses of corned hake and the countless ways to make hake fishballs and related delights. We had a good supply of corned hake, and the gulls were gone when we spied Mr. Thomas and his sloop in the gut. The gulls had taken care of every last hake that we hadn't. Mr. Thomas said he could have got rid of ten times as much hake, and as nobody else had brought any in he presumed the wash-up had been strictly for us. He looked at the supply of hake we'd corned and said it looked good, and then he asked, "Did anybody think to save some fish for supper?"

Chapter 18

HISTORY AND
THE FRENCH COW

Mr. Thomas liked to talk, talked well, and when he'd start to answer one of my father's questions he'd sound like a school teacher for a while, and then he'd ease off and sound like a Maine lobster catcher. My father said he could listen to Mr. Thomas all night, and my mother said, "I was afraid we'd have to!" This was not meant to be unkind; my mother liked to hear his stories, too. What my mother was thinking about was the way Mr. Thomas would bring our evening sessions to an end. Flip hour was the beginning, and whether we ate at one house or divided by families, we'd come together after supper. Then, as Mr. Thomas would be talking along about whatever it was, he'd suddenly stop, stand up, say "Good night!" and go to bed.

That was that. Then, next evening at flip hour Mr. Thomas would find the right moment, and he would simply say, "Now, to resume. . ." and he would pick up where he left off. That morning that left all the beached-out hake on our shore turned into a long day, and ended with our hearing the story of salt. Mr. Thomas said good-night and went to bed, and the next evening he said, "Well, to resume. . ."

That day had been the first of a "three-day blow." We'd have several of those every summer at Morning River. A dry

73

west, or northwest, wind would rise in the night and continue for three days. It didn't bring rain, except maybe short squalls, but it would kick up the ocean so nobody used a boat and often-times the mail boat to Monhegan would cancel a trip. Ashore, it was uncomfortable to do anything, unless in the shop, so it was usual to lay odd jobs aside until we had a three-day blow. Our finest summer days would be those that followed such a blow. The air would be fresh and clean, and everything would be dusted. This one had been that kind of a day, and the saying was that a man could spit half-way to Spain, so Mr. Thomas had gone up in the sawmill loft and brought down a fish flake. Several were up there, taken apart for storage, and they were left over from the days when Morning River Farm slack-salted its own fish, perhaps to sell, but certainly for home use. This gave Mr. Thomas something to do out of the wind, and we learned it would be an exhibit for his evening lecture.

When the time came, flip hour was devoted to comments about the day's stiff wind, and how we could expect two more days of it, and after Mrs. Crowthers had served one of her shepherd pies, and we-all had polished it away, Mr. Thomas said, "And now, to resume, this here is a fish flake probably made by Jules Marcoux going-on a hundred years ago, and before it was laid away somebody probably scraped off the fish scales. This is the thing that set out in the wind and sun to dry the salt fish and except to throw rocks I have no idea what they did about the shitpokes. If you'll excuse me! I'm sorry! Force of habit!"

(Mr. Thomas was clearly embarrassed. Maine lobstermen use that word for the common seagull, and it's possible not too many of them know that a shitpoke is not a gull, but is one of the herons. I think a green heron, but not a gull. It is not, however, a serious error. A gull hovers over fishing boats, and becomes a nuisance until the word is more apt for a gull than it is for the heron.)

Having recovered his social composure, Mr. Thomas continued. "Time was, places along the Maine coast were rated by the number of fish flakes being used. Portland was called

Falmouth and had about 700. Monhegan Island had maybe twice that. Biggest batch was on Fisherman's Island over Boothbay way. Then, down east, the Frenchmen had their places in Nova Scotia and New Brunswick, and then at Frenchman's Bay and all along there. How come we find names like Isle au Haut, Jesuit Point, St. Savior? (Mr. Thomas said, "*Eel uh Hut!*") Now, comes the difference. The Englishmen came here pounding the Bible and making great cry about their importance, and they cheated the Indians and told them to move along, and before long they generated enough bad feeling to last a couple of hundred years. It got so they didn't dast go ashore to 'tend their flakes without some warships and the militia, and they began shipping a bad grade of fish. They put fish in brine and shipped it in barrels, and if it didn't get green slime on it, it took on a smell and a flavor, and by the time it got to England it would gag a backhouse rat. If you'll excuse me again.

"But the French! They asked the Indians to come and have pea soup, and to sing in church, and they made a big hit. They even gave the Indian a honk now and then. So the Frenchmen could go ashore without setting off any massacres, and they gave their flakes all the sun and wind the fish needed, and some of them even married squaws that would dress fish and drive seagulls. So what happened was two very different kinds of salt fish, and it didn't take people long to tell one from the other. The French kind was the hard cure, and the English kind was the soft cure. The French kind was the good kind. The English kind, soft and flabby, would turn brown and cooked mushy, and when even the English people wouldn't use it, they did what every country does when it has already lost one—they started a war.

"The first thing to do was to get rid of the Frenchmen, so they sent a warship up from Virginia, and they began this little matter by attacking the Frenchmen over at St. Savior, Bar Harbor way. Yes, they did! The Frenchmen, cutting fish and minding their own business, didn't know the English were mad at them, so they were some surprised when this warship appeared, shooting cannon at them, and I guess they did what any sensible person would do—they high-tailed it for the woods. So the English came in, and after they shot things up they stole everything they could crowd aboard the warship and then set fire to what was left. Nice people and a pleasant afternoon.

"There were two priests at St. Savior. One of them took a cannon ball in the leg, but the other one got his leg out of the way. The English took the one that didn't get hurt and took him down to Virginia. Oh, yes—I forgot to speak of the cow. The Frenchmen had a cow at St. Savior, and the Englishmen took her aboard and she went to Virginia with the priest and all the other stolen stuff."

Han spoke up to say, "I thought you were going to forget to tell about the cow!"

Mr. Thomas said, "No, I got her in all right," and to the rest of us he said, "Han likes the part about the cow, and when she was smaller she'd always ask if French cows talk French."

Han said, "We had a French family spend one summer on Monhegan, and I'd hear them talking and wonder if the cow would understand them."

Mr. Thomas said, "England was very proud of this attack on the French, except for the part about kidnapping the priest. That violated all decency, and orders came by the next boat from London that the priest was to be treated kind and proper, and he was to be compensated for any inconveniences, and he was to be returned to St. Savior immediately. An apology was already on its way to the Society of Jesus."

Now Han broke in again! "But they couldn't send the priest back right away, because he was the only person at Jamestown that could speak French, and they needed him to take care of that cow!"

"That's the story," said Mr. Thomas. "They had to keep him in Virginia until that cow learned to speak English. But joking aside, I did see a piece in a Sunday paper some years back, and it said the first milking cow in America was brought to Virginia in 1613. Which is not quite true. She was a French-speaking cow that was stolen from Maine."

I guess this seemed like a good place to bring a pleasant evening to an end, so Mr. Thomas pushed the salt-fish flake against the wall with his foot, stood up, and said, "Good night!"

And went to bed.

Chapter 19

ABOUT
THE SALT

That hake day was a long day. Mrs. Thomas made creamed fresh hake, and both families had supper at the Marcoux house. Mrs. Crowthers, thus having the evening off, paid dutiful attention to instructions from Mrs. Thomas, and allowed she could now make creamed fresh hake, which wasn't a difficult dish for anything so good. My father had become greatly interested in the whole subject of salt fish, and kept asking questions of Mr. Thomas all evening. "How did the old fish cutters of early Maine keep the seagulls from swarming in and stealing all the fish laid out on the drying racks?" Mr. Thomas had a way of crinkling his forehead and saying, "That's a good question," and then sitting back to think up his answer. But that question stumped him. "I don't know," he said. His mother, he told us, liked to salt-slack enough pollock for the winter, and had enough old sheets and blankets to cover what few fish she split. "But when you stop and think of the hundreds of flakes exposed in early times all along the Maine coast, you realize what a poor job the historians do.

"I was a plagu-ed nuisance in school days," Mr. Thomas said, "when I'd up and ask some question my teacher couldn't answer. She'd do the only thing she could; she'd tell me to look it up. And where would you look it up? The school had three books to look things up in—the dictionary, a circular on the Hartford make-and-break one cylinder engine, and a book on what to do until the doctor comes. I don't know what they did to fend off the gulls. I never thought about it. Now that you ask, I'd like to know."

Mr. Thomas stood up, moved his chair back from the table so it would tip against the wall, and sat down. "A very good question," he said. Then he was quite ready, and he began. "I did ask about salt. Salt I can talk about all night. What would you like to know about salt?"

As the years raced along and summer followed summer at Morning River Farm, we all looked forward to the occasions when Mr. Thomas would arrange himself and offer to be the speaker of the evening. My father relished the way Mr. Thomas handled his narrative, and the next morning would find a way to review it for me. Did I see how he brought the subject up; did I see his indirections to bring directions out; did I get the laugh in his understatement? I began to realize that I did, indeed, notice a craftsmanship but didn't always appreciate it until my father explained. I just knew Mr. Thomas was fun to listen to. My father said, "Tell us about salt."

Mr. Thomas began. "It was the usual thing. We'd be studying something in school, and I'd get to wondering. All this big business about our North Atlantic Fisheries was right at home to us kids on Monhegan. When we heard that the Mayflower, bringing the Pilgrims, laid over at Monhegan long enough to catch some codfish, we weren't studying history so much as we were hearing about ourselves and how we were right smack-dab on the way and were in the codfish business. So the first thing the Pilgrims did when they got here was to fish! We kids lapped up the Pilgrim story. And so one day the teacher was telling how the boats came here to get fish and Monhegan Island was just one of the places they loaded. I suppose we all knew something was lacking, but I was the troublesome boy that couldn't keep his mouth shut.

"So I'd ask questions, and the teacher wanted to wring my neck. These fish, I asked, had to be caught. Who caught them? Must have been a lot of people around here dressing fish and rubbing salt, and—since you mention it—fighting seagulls. My mother used to throw rocks at them. She was a sweet woman that loved everything, and she'd connect with a seagull and jump up and down and clap her hands and laugh like a hyena. Raccoons and seagulls. My mother hated them.

"So we were getting all this stuff in school about the importance of salt fish to Monhegan and all along Nova Scotia, and not one word did any of us hear about where these people got all the salt they were using. We don't have any salt in these parts. Every grain of salt I buy for my lobster bait comes from somewhere. The train brings it to Rockland, and I get it from a dealer. The teacher would tell us to look it up. That was no good. My mother got interested, and she told the teacher to look it up for the whole bunch of us. She said even the Bible tells about saltmines, but doesn't mention Monhegan Island. My mother did have a comical bent at times. But I have to say that we never found out about salt. History books kept pushing salt fish, but no historian ever stopped to wonder about salt."

My father said, "I thought you were going to tell us where we got salt."

"I am, I am! I found out. But it was a long time after I got out of school, and no thanks to any teacher or any history book. I was lobstering, and buying salt, and one day at Port Clyde I chanced to be talking to the Shurtleff salt man, and I asked him. You know what he said?"

My father said, "He said, 'That's a good question!'"

"That's right! He said he could answer me, but that the Shurtleff people paid a high-priced press agent to sit around, and he would have this press agent write to me with full details. Which the man did. I was still little more than a youngster, and I got this letter addressed to Mister!

"He said some of the salt mines used in the early American fisheries are still in use today, and it might be possible that salt I buy for my lobster bait comes from the same place in Spain that sold salt to the Mayflower. The Mayflower had made voyages to Maine for the fish before she was chartered to bring the Pilgrims. He told me a boat coming to Maine for fish would go to Spain first and load salt in ballast and get good tariff for it over here.

"Then, he said some salt was made here in America by boiling down ocean water. That kind of salt brought about fifteen pennies a bushel. I tried that. I got a bucket set up on some flat rocks, and I'd fill the bucket with sea water and then make a driftwood fire. It took more time than I expected, but I got some salt all right. It was brownish, and tasted like salt but it made fish mushy. There was something the man didn't tell me. But that's how the people around here got their salt, and I always thought it was a good thing to know. It ought to be in a schoolbook."

My father said, "So should the story of how your mother threw rocks at seagulls."

"It should, it should! But as long as we let the historians write our history books, we'll have curious little shavers asking questions. Good night."

Chapter 20

THE BLUEFISH SPEECH

The summer of the corned hake was one of our best at Morning River Farm, perhaps because it gave us so many things to remember. For one thing, it gave my father things to do, and drew him away from his sworn intention to sit around and do nothing and enjoy his vacation. He began contemplating the improbability that salt fish was what settled North America and brought on a prosperity unequaled anywhere else. And, best of all, Morning River had been plunk in the middle of it. The multitude had truly been fed. Back in Philadelphia my father began reminding people that the sacred codfish hangs in the assembly hall of the Massachusetts General Court in Boston, and that when they were starving down at Plymouth the Pilgrims went up to his place in Maine to get food. Fish, that was. Might have been corned hake. He climbed over things stored in the sawmill and brought out another of the Jules Marcoux fish flakes. Mr. Thomas helped him assemble it, and then he scraped and sandpapered it, and varnished it, and it became a bookcase in his law office in Philadelphia. The wood is beautiful. And people who admire the bookcase may notice that the first book they see is a history of the State of Maine by John S. C. Abbott, published in Augusta, Maine, in 1802. My father paid twenty-five cents for it at an auction in Virginia.

Then my father developed a lecture that he gave to clubs and study groups. He had several titles for the talk, but the speech was always the same. Most often, his audiences wanted to hear "The Truth About Those Pilgrims." He'd tell them that when the history books say the Pilgrims subsisted on shellfish, it means they lived on clams. This explains the sour expression on all the portraits of Elder Brewster. "That's not piety," he'd say, "that's clams." People were amazed that a speech about salt fish could keep a Philadelphia audience rapt for a full hour, but his did. I went with him one time when he spoke to an insurance convention. He told how Han had cleaned his fish for him. I was on our wharf at Morning River the day Han had given him her rousing brush-off on that subject. It had to do with the bluefish.

The day before, Mr. Thomas had noticed a fish break water in the gut, and he said, "Little action out there!" He had then gone to set a trotline. A trotline is anchored on both ends, one ashore, and you don't need to attend it. The baited hook is off where you think the fish is, and this time Mr. Thomas suspected it was a good bluefish feeding off some kayaks. Usually thought of as a sport fish, the bluefish is good eating. He has sharp teeth, and can bite off a line if hooked, so a metal wire is best for a leader. Mr. Thomas left his trotline out all night, and in the morning had a decent bluefish. Big enough for both families at supper. Mr. Thomas dressed the fish and set his trotline again.

The next morning we had another, and with his new interest in the history of salt fish my father decided to corn the bluefish and see how it came out. Mr. Thomas said, "Never heard of corned bluefish."

Han very willingly dressed out the bluefish, and in doing so she said, "I think it's time you learned to gut your own fish!" It was said with a giggle, no offense meant and none taken. My father said, "Long as you don't mind, I don't have to!"

That did it! Han stuck the knife in the cutting board,

walked over to my father, wiped her hands on his shirt, took one of his hands in hers, and began: "Now, look you, Mister! I gut fish because I know how, and it needs doing. But don't you go around telling your Philadelphia friends I don't mind! I do mind. I hate cleaning fish! If I was you, and I had a girl to clean my fish, I'd be glad, but I wouldn't go around telling people she likes to do it! So, Mister Man! Is there some way I can get you to clean a fish?"

My father looked over at me, and then he reached for Han. He pulled her by both shoulders so he could kiss her on the forehead, and then he pulled the knife out of the board and said, "Show me."

Han showed him.

That evening as I sat in the audience and heard my father give his talk on salt fish, and other things, I sat up straight and realized I wasn't in Philadelphia at all. I was on the wharf at Morning River, hearing Han's voice as she told my father how to get a bluefish backbone out in one piece. I heard her saying, "Now, you leave the head. It's no good, so you heave it overboard just as far as you can. There's a splash, and before you get your hand down an eel has it. There's eels in here three feet long and growing. Buggers to skin!"

Yes, I did. Absorbed by my memories, I was there on the wharf, and I ducked when my father made believe throw the bluefish head to the eels.

The salt fish summer was notable, but except for the history we learned and the memories we cherish, it didn't run over into the next year. There was always something else. When we came to Morning River again, the wind had blown away a sign Han and I made and nailed to a spile on the wharf:

SALT FISH WORKS
Supreme Corned Hake

Order Early For
Holiday Giving

Nobody ever ordered any of our salt fish and we never sold any. Cousin Snood cured some fish over on Monhegan, and he had the business tied up anyway. But my father always took some of his own cure back to Philadelphia in the fall and his friends liked to get some. He gave it away. He'd say, "Everybody asks why the stores don't sell good salt fish now, but I wonder if anybody would buy it?" Still, three or four times a summer we'd have salt fish suppers at Morning River, and while Mrs. Thomas always cooked them, Mrs. Crowthers ate her share.

Chapter 21

OUR
SHIPWRECK

A shipwreck is a terrible thing, but when we had our only shipwreck at Morning River Farm we didn't know anything about it until the next day. One of the pretty Boston boats piled up on a squishy, squidgey clam flat on the ocean side of Big Razor Island and like a fly on sticky fly paper remained attached. Actually, the Boston boats came and went every day, but they were usually offshore so we didn't see them. Sometimes we'd see their lights at night. When we did get a good look at one, she was always beautiful in her white paint, and majestic in the way she came from one way and went the other. When one of them blew her stack to clean out coal soot, a black cloud would hang all over the ocean. Mr. Thomas told us that in the winter the soot would settle, depending on the wind, and often the new snow would be dirty in minutes. Mr. Thomas wasn't kindly disposed toward steamships, and power boats of any kind, and he knew all the disparaging remarks to be made about the captains on the Boston boats. We never knew which of the several Boston boats went aground on Razor Island, but Mr. Thomas said the skipper was probably having his teatime nap and his butler didn't wake him in time to blow his whistle. He "guessed" the boat was fifteen miles off course.

It was late afternoon but by no means dark when the vessel went aground, at just about a three-quarter tide. The boat was not damaged and nobody was hurt, and the captain decided there was nothing to do but wait for tugboats to pull her off. Bound for Boston, the boat would be missed when she didn't reach Bath on schedule, and soon after that the Coast Guard would arrive from, probably, Boothbay Harbor.

We could have seen the boat stuck in the mud, but didn't chance to look, and the next thing I knew I woke up when my father asked, "What's going on around here, anyway?" It was daylight, but the sun wasn't up yet, and I heard a jumble of men's voices. I didn't make out any words, just a jumble and when I looked out my window I saw Mr. Thomas come out of the Marcoux house and start across to our wharf. It was the three men on the wharf that I'd heard talking. Then, at about the same time, my father and I saw the Boston boat over on Razor Island, a black shadow against the coming sunrise, and to me she looked ten times her size. My father announced, to the world in general, "Boat's come ashore!" So we had a shipwreck.

We never knew what happened, but evidently nothing did. The boat's failure to appear did not alarm anybody and the Coast Guard was not alerted. Passengers on the steamer hadn't felt any bump, and probably Mr. Thomas was correct and the captain was napping. But at daylight three crew members lowered one of the steamer's great lifeboats and rowed it from the ocean side over to our side of Razor Island. Our houses could be seen from the boat. The men tied the lifeboat to our wharf and came ashore, expecting we'd have a telephone. Then we all had a conference.

Mr. Thomas sprinkled in some remarks about steamboat people, and suggested we have a mug up and then he would take the men back to the steamboat, towing their lifeboat, and if the Coast Guard hadn't appeared by that time he'd go with his sloop to either Boothbay or Port Clyde. This would also offer a chance to check the steamship out and see if any ladies had fainted.

Well, it wasn't winter, so nobody was going to be frozen to any masts, and as the sea was what Mr. Thomas rated as a glassy-arse calm, there wouldn't be any bounding billows to smash the steamer to shreds on the rocks.

By this time Han and I were at our Croze Nest and had the steamer in our spyglass. She was white now, as the sun was over her, and pathetic sitting there helpless. We couldn't see anybody aboard her. It wasn't long before the others, lacking only Mr. Thomas, were in the Croze Nest with us, and there never was a finer place to watch a shipwreck. But soon Mr. Thomas's sloop hove in view on the other side of Big Razor, and we followed her along until she came to the beached steamer. Now the sloop passed out of our sight, the steamship between, and we had to imagine what was going on.

Then the Coast Guard arrived. One from the east, one from the west, and both of them went behind the steamship to join, we presumed, the Thomas sloop. But Mr. Thomas, alone in his sloop, shortly appeared and went west to go around the end of the island and come to Morning River.

The show was just starting. When Mr. Thomas and his sloop appeared in our spyglass, the sloop looked as big as six Boston boats, and Han and I went to the wharf to tie her for the night.

Mr. Thomas said tugboats were on their way, and the plan was to pull the steamship free without taking off the passengers. If they could free her with one pull, and Mr. Thomas believed they could, she could continue to Bath or Portland and the passengers would be transferred to another boat. The steamship had enough food and nobody seemed disturbed by the misadventure. If the wind didn't rise, there need be no anxiety. Mr. Thomas said it seemed to be a very cheerful wreck.

And that's the way things turned out. Two tugs came, one from Bath and one from Belfast, and after a look-see it was decided one would pull and one push. Water under the steamship's prow was deep enough. This was great to watch from the Croze Nest, and as Mr. Thomas was now with us we had the benefit of his opinions about steamboat captains who run ashore.

The tug that was to push arranged her hemp mats and nuzzled close. The other had its long line positioned. At the moment, Mrs. Crowthers was at the eye-piece of our telescope, and she saw the hand wave that was a signal to go to work. She screamed, "There you go!"

And they went. Mrs. Crowthers saw through the spy-glass, but the rest of us used the window. The pusher tug set up a considerable wake, but the puller strained steadily and her line seemed to stretch somewhat. "She's moving," said Mrs. Crowthers.

Out she came. The tug that was pushing merely stopped pushing, made a turn, and kept on going to Belfast. The other tug retrieved her long hawser, tooted her horn, and went to Bath. The Boston boat took a time to get up steam, and then she left. The other folks left our Croze Nest and Han and I put the cover over the spyglass. Mrs. Crowthers, pleading it was time to start supper (in Philadelphia she would say 'dinner'), had gone on ahead with the remark, "Think of all the people in this world who never saw a shipwreck!"

Chapter 22

SUNDAY SCHOOL

At home in Philadelphia, I was faithful with Sunday School. This was to please my mother. But at Morning River Farm in Maine there was no way she could think of to cause me to please her, although I remember the day she asked Mrs. Thomas about the *Sunbeam*. This was the vessel of the Maine Seacoast Missionary Society, and we never had the honor of having her put in at our wharf. Possibly my mother hoped the *Sunbeam* might confer special dispensation and come on the Lord's Day to bring me Christian instruction. But I lacked that until September when I was back in Philadelphia. There was an exception. Surprising everybody, my father arranged a Sunday School class, which he conducted, right in our kitchen, and it began right after Mrs. Crowthers crumbed the table.

Mrs. Crowthers fed songbirds. My father, who indulged her in this at home, put his foot down at the thought of getting bird food to Morning River. They've got wings, he said, let 'em fly up to Bangor and bring back their own grub. So table scraps were important to Mrs. Crowthers and her friends, and she'd brush the table vigorously.

On this Sunday morning my father stood up so Mrs. Crowthers could get past him to brush, and he said to me, "I suppose you do miss Sunday School while you're here?"

I said not so I lost any sleep about it.

"I know," he said, "but Sunday School is not a complete waste of time. There are those who consider the Bible a dialectic achievement. I'm not about to belittle it on a Sunday morning. So let's have a Sunday School lesson. You stay here and I'll be back in a twinkle."

I didn't know that my father had paid any attention to the books upstairs. He came to Morning River, he said, to get away from books. But he came down to the kitchen again with two books and a piece of paper torn from his legal pad. "Here we are!" he said. He handed me the piece of yellow paper, and on it he'd written:

PISS PISSETH

He handed me one of the books. It was the Bible. The other book he held up for me to see.

He said, "In Sunday School, did they tell you about the concordance? I didn't expect so. Well, this is a concordance to the Holy Bible. It tells you all the words in the Bible, and where to find them. If you look up fire, this tells you every place in the Bible where you'll find fire. Now, you look up what's on this paper, and read what the Bible says about it, and I'll give you fifteen minutes. I have an idea your Sunday School teacher back home never told you people in the Bible went to the toilet!"

He rubbed the top of my head as he left the kitchen.

No, nobody had told me that, and I did not believe I was going to find piss in the Bible. It wasn't like my father, at least, and it shouldn't be like the Bible. But there it was! Piss against the wall!

My father gave me my fifteen minutes. I had torn the scrap of note paper in small pieces, and used it for book marks. I had found the references and I had looked up and read several.

But my father didn't ask what I'd found. He said, "The Bible says to get wisdom, but to get understanding. You want to understand that all men like to have sons. Little girls are all right, and are nice to have, but they don't stand up and squirt against the wall. In those old battles of Bible times, the first way to hurt a man was to do away with his boy children. One reason, the best reason, we read these old stories is to learn how they lived. You had a fight with somebody, so you killed his boys. Girls didn't count. Now, here you are at Morning River Farm, and you've been spending a lot of time with Mr. Thomas, who doesn't have a boy child. I guess that the more he sees of you, the more he thinks he was short changed. Now, again, Han is a dear child, and Mr. Thomas knows that, but he still doesn't have a boy. There's a whole great lot deep-down-inside here, and it doesn't show, but Mr. Thomas keeps thinking about it, and you and I need to understand and help him along. I guess what I mean is that you want to be kind to Mr. Thomas, and without going overboard be a little bit his piss against the wall. Do I make sense?"

I said yes, but I was to think about this Sunday School lesson a good deal before I understood it all that much. Then, too, I misdirected myself by wondering what my summers would be like if Han was able to do what I could do. Then, I'd laugh at myself because as an island girl Han could do so many, many things a boy from Philadelphia had yet to know about. But I told my mother at suppertime that my father was a good Sunday School teacher.

Chapter 23

BROOK
TROUT

After we had some time to get acquainted with our Morning River neighbors, most of them fifteen miles away, my father said to Mr. Thomas one morning, "I suppose your rascal Cousin Snood is the most frequently arrested poacher in Maine's seventeen counties?" Mr. Thomas, under no illusions about his cousin, said, "Sixteen counties. We used to have seventeen, but Cousin Snood stole one back when he was a boy." All the same, Cousin Snood was the favorite neighbor to Han and me, and he never showed up but something wonderful happened. It was Cousin Snood who set things up for my first "trout hunt," and nobody can ever do anything nicer for a person than connect him to a Maine trout while the iron frypan is hot. Han was Cousin Snood's agent in this memorable event.

Han had never fished for trout, and as an island girl knew nothing about mainland brooks and about Morning River in particular. When Cousin Snood heard that the Thomas family would be spending their summers at Morning River, he said Morning River was the best trout stream in Maine, unless you wanted to go three hundred miles into the wilderness and live in a tent. He told Han, "I'll take you there and show you where my rain barrel is!" This he did, so later on when the time came and we had a "trout day," Han took me to see and do what Cousin Snood had taken care of.

I think it was during our second summer, but it might have been our third (things run together!) and we had experienced the several kinds of fish chowders and stews. Lobster, crab, clam, scallop, cunner, haddock, pollock, and also cod. Han and I had been jigging for mackerel from our sailing dory, and she had somehow found a codfish. It was Cousin Snood who said, "You ain't et a real fish chowder till you've stuck your teeth into one made of trout." So then Han said we'd watch the signs for the next trout day.

Cousin Snood had readied Han for all this foolishness. Maine people, I found, don't bother to try a trout brook until these signs are propitious. If the signs are right, you've got a "trout day." If you go fishing on a trout day, and the trout aren't biting, then the signs were wrong. Either that, or it simply wasn't a trout day. Cousin Snood told me once that the only true signs are "in the belly." If a trout is hungry, he'll bite. All the other signs can fail. And all I'm going to say is that Han wouldn't take me to catch a trout until she was satisfied the signs were right. We had heard, as one of the Elzada legends, that Madame Elzada would put the frypan on to heat, dump in her diced salt pork, and then step out the back door to catch her breakfast trout off the steps. She paid no attention to signs. And Cousin Snood said never to catch your second trout until you'd fried and eaten the first. What about signs? But Han waited two days for the signs to take shape.

It was in August, Cousin Snood said he believed sea-run trout still came into Morning River to spawn, but you wouldn't see one until the middle of August. Meat was pinkier. And in August trout are brighter colored as spawning time approaches. No other fish, even those meant for fishbowls, Cousin Snood said, can match spots with a brookie in the fall. And didn't I, all innocent, ask Han what this spawning was all about?

We did not have any store-bought rods. We had the cunner lines Mr. Thomas had wound on little pieces of wood, with shingle nail sinkers and small hooks. Han said we'd find the maple poles Cousin Snood had cut where they'd stashed them, and we'd tie our cunner lines to them. But no shingle nails. "You'll see why," Han told me. And I did. A couple of summers after that my father brought his expensive bamboo fly-rod and like Madame Elzada he cast into the pool by the back door. A trout that my father saw just once struck, smashed the rod tip and snapped the line.

Han said we'd need a few things, so I got two clam hods from the sawmill. She put in soap and a towel, a square of fat salt pork from the cellar, a frypan and flipper, some bread and two cuts of cake wrapped in napkins, and a fork apiece. Pepper and salt. Two tin clam-bake cups. And a hatchet. And a couple of fillet knives. One clam hod would do, but we each took one. With our wound-up cunner lines in our pockets, Han and I were ready to make my first trout hunt.

My father said, "I take it the signs are right?"

Han said, "Never better."

It was a beautiful day, but hazy so we didn't have a high, blue sky. Han said Cousin Snood favored some overcast. A dull day is best for trout. But it was cool for August, and we had plenty of goldenrod along the river to warn us that fall was on the way. In the old days there had been a farming road along Morning River, and although grown up to weeds and bushes lately, it was still there and walking was easy. We scared up some partridges, and also some woodcock.

The big bunny swamp that feeds the cataract by our back door, and then forms Morning River, is not on low land. The river might have flowed five hundred feet and gone into tidewater, but it turned west instead and ran back towards the maple sugar hills. Then it made a horseshoe turn and came all the way back. A good five hundred acres of farmland lay within the horseshoe curve, all of it cultivated in the days of Jabez Knight and Jules Marcoux. When the sawmill was built, the river became the millpond, above the dam, and over the dam and through the spillway Morning River found our salt-water estuary and the

95

sea. The trout pool that Cousin Snood had shown to Han was right at the crook of the horseshoe, and was his "rain barrel." "Like shooting fish in a rain barrel" is the saying. He said cold-water springs from the hills beyond fed into it to make it ideal for trout. A stone fireplace from long ago was waiting for us, and a little shelter to keep firewood dry. Also, two maple saplings, limber and lithe, leaning against a tree; our trout rods.

"Now," said Han, and she became the school teacher again, showing me, the stranger, all the things I didn't know and which, in this instance, she didn't know either until Cousin Snood had recently instructed.

"Always leave as much firewood as you burn, and a little more," she said, passing me the hatchet from the clam hod. "Be sure to leave chips and bark for kindling. Put a stone on the bark so it won't blow away."

Being no great shakes as a lumberjack, it took me a while to cut a couple of maple saplings and put them in the shelter, and Han took care of kindling twigs. She also got things laid out to cook the trout we hadn't caught yet. I did hope the signs were dependable. It came time to start our fire.

"Did you bring any matches?" Han asked.

"No."

Han properly allowed me to savor the sunken, all-gone stupid moment this ancient State o'Maine jest always visits on the gullible guest from away, and then she ran her hand in her shirt pocket to get her waterproofed bottle of waxed matches.

Han said, "I've been looking forward all morning to pulling that on you! Don't ever again forget matches. Cousin Snood says it's a foolish man who freezes to death in a wooden country. Don't ever do it!"

So we soon had embers, and Han diced the salt pork and put it in the fry-pan. It started to sizzle. She had saved out one little cube of pork, and now she put it on the cunner hook and handed me my maple switch, all ready for the big adventure. She said, "Now, all the signs are perfect. First, you spit on your bait for luck, and then you let the line run down in that little V by the rock. Your trout is waiting. And don't expect a diddy-diddy-do like a cunner. You'll see, but be ready and don't let him drag you around the pool." My piece of pork was right by that little V.

A couple of years before that, in Philadelphia, some city workers were going to do some blasting for water pipes near my school and our teacher asked if it would be safe if we children went into the schoolyard to watch. The man said certainly, and when the time came we marched out and lined up where the man told us to, and he said to be ready for a noise and not to be frightened. It did make a noise, and it blew mud and water into the air, and we were all a little frightened.

That's what it's like to catch a trout in Morning River.

The trout that was waiting for me made his presence known, and I saw him come out of the water, throwing a spout into the air, and when he went back into the hole he'd made in the water I could see those beautiful spots that brighten in August. My line went tight, and my maple withe doubled. Han, standing behind me, was yelling advice, and in just about three seconds had said, "Keep the line tight!" seventy-nine times. I did notice that the bend of the maple was keeping the line tight when I didn't, and I was doing rather well just to hang onto the pole.

Han quieted down and came to stand by me and offer further advice in a confidential manner. Cousin Snood had done well, and I was getting the good of it. The trout went up and down, over, and around-about, and gradually slowed to maybe eighty miles an hour. Han said, "Bring him in!" and she slipped a finger into his gill and had him between her knees. "Get me one!" she said, and with the same piece of pork still on the hook, the little V by the rock gave me a second. Han had the first dressed, and she showed me how to dress the second. The salt pork in the frypan was turning crisp, and our embers were perfect.

Han told me, "Cook slow with small heat or trout will curl up in the pan. And Cousin Snood says to catch and eat all you want, but never more than one at a time."

These trout were measured by a stick, and then we put the stick to a tape back at the house, and they were twins at eleven-and-a-half inches. Nice pound trout. We took one more apiece for our lunch, which Han caught and I dressed, and after we rinsed the pan and plates we took a dozen more to be carried home for a trout chowder. But not for that evening. Cousin Snood had said that two days are needed to make a decent trout soup. One to get it in the right direction, and a second day to head it off at the table.

It has always seemed implausible to me that I could spend so many happy summers on the Atlantic Coast of Maine, with hake washing up on the beach and cunners and mackerel and pollock by the pail and clams for the digging, and lobsters galore, and my richest piscatorial moment was when that trout exploded into view in that little V by the rock. A fresh-water fish?

Chapter 24

FISH WARDENS

My father had hoped I would spend a lot of my summer time with Mr. Thomas. I could go with him to haul and be exposed to his knowledge and down-Maine philosophy, and would learn to sail his sloop, and increase in wisdom. Several things defeated this hope. First, the State of Maine jealously guards its lobster fishery, and as an attorney my father quickly said it would take a Philadelphia Lawyer to figure some things out. A youngster from away can presumably go out in a lobster boat with a Maine lobster catcher, but if he even looks at a bait iron he is already breaking the law. He can ride, but he mustn't touch anything. But we had no tangle over that, because the Monhegan Island lobstermen work under a special law and their fishing season ends the last of May. Mr. Thomas would be done fishing a few days before we arrived for the summer, and we'd go home in September. He couldn't fish again until January. My father said this made conservation sense, but as he understood things, I could go haul with Mr. Thomas, were he to haul, if he got a special permit for his boat, not for me. Anyway, I never did haul with Mr. Thomas.

For his summer clam bakes, Mr. Thomas couldn't catch

the lobsters fed to his summer tourists. He had to buy them from dealers and they had to be caught by mainland fishermen, not islanders. So he had a "car," which is a slatted crate made for holding lobsters, moored in Razor Island Gut right off our wharf, and he had to have a permit for that and it was subject to inspection by the Sea & Shore Fisheries wardens. Maine lobsters must be so long, and can't be too short, and possession of oversize and undersize lobsters is not only a criminal offense, but it makes the offender look very bad among his friends and relatives. An honest man takes no chances, and Mr. Thomas never did. However, it was the custom for the fish wardens to come to Morning River Farm periodically and inspect his car officiously with every indication that they expected for certain-sure to find him harboring some shorts. Mr. Thomas would grin, and he and the wardens would squat on their heels and talk things over for so long we wondered how they kept their balance. Mr. Thomas and the wardens were such good and long-time friends that we surmised the officers would look the other way if they found a short in his car, but Mr. Thomas said, "Don't you believe it! They'd have me in court and call all the newspapers!"

The two fish wardens who thus came regularly to Morning River were very much special people. Han did, but I didn't know who they were. She had looked up and said, "Here's the *Maine!*" when the whistle blew, and when the boat got close enough I saw two policemen. A city boy, I had no way to tell a cop from a warden, and Han's evidence of joy caused me wonder. She was glad, and ran towards our wharf. The boat, which was the *Maine*, was not small, and I found out later could come up our estuary to the wharf only at high tide. Eighty-five feet long (I also learned later) the *Maine* was the official state patrol boat of the Sea & Shore Fisheries Department. She was under the command of Captain Clarence Meservey, and Han introduced him to me with becoming dignity, even as he had an arm around her shoulder and was hugging her to his hip. That summer we were nine. Then I met Engineer Clayton Simmons, a younger man, who didn't show the same avuncular affection for Han, but shook hands gravely and asked for her health. Engineer Simmons was also the mate, assistant sea-going warden, cook, and chore-boy. Captain Meservey wore his warden's cap squarely level, precisely fore-and-aft, and suitable to his lawful importance. Mate Simmons wore his a bit askew, proving there are some things not to be taken wholly seriously.

Maine has other fish wardens, all along the coast from Kittery to Eastport, each with his own district, but just the one boat. Besides cruising the entire coast, back and forth, the *Maine* also serves in semi-official ways, such as taking big-shot guests of the governor on clam bakes and fishing trips, and perhaps finding a cool sea breeze for the Senate Appropriations Committee on a hot August afternoon. The *Maine* has accommodations for maybe ten guests. On this first occasion, when Han introduced me, Captain Meservey automatically said, "Welcome aboard!" and he and Mate Simmons left the *Maine*, tied to our wharf, to Han and me and walked over to the Marcoux house. They would have a mug-up with Mr. and Mrs. Thomas, and with my mother and father as soon as Mr. Thomas could walk up to the other house and bring them back. And Han took me up the ladder-steps aboard the *Maine*, where we went in the wheelhouse to the chart room and found a plate of cry-baby cookies on the table. Cook Simmons always baked a pan of cry-babies for Han, either at Monhegan or at (now!) Morning River. A cry-baby cookie, I now knew, is a double sugar cookie with raisins between. Han and I sat at the chart table and ate some, saving others for later, while the mug-up went on, and I don't remember that any effort whatever was made to inspect our lobster car for shorts.

Since the *Maine* was always on a prowl mission, seeking whom it might arrest, it never came at an expected time. So it always blew its air horn and alerted us. Over the years we swapped a good many mug-ups for cry-baby cookies until we heard the *Maine* had been sold for a small craft and, I think, captain and mate had retired.

Mr. Thomas told us Captain Meservey was a Scot and

liked his oatmeal porridge, whereas Cook Simmons detested oatmeal and refused to cook it for him. Unable to agree about this, the two would prepare separate breakfasts each morning, making sarcastic remarks as they collided about the galley, and then rising from table to get the *Maine* underway in hearty good fellowship. Cook Simmons would, however, open a porthole on the windward side to air out the galley and rid it of that terrible stench from the god-awful Caledonian porridge. Mr. Thomas said he knew for a fact that Captain Meservey would sail the *Maine* well out of her jurisdiction and into the Bay of Fundy where he could buy honest ground oatmeal instead of the rolled oats that had taken over the market in Maine. Cook Simmons, Mr. Thomas said, never mentioned this if he were keeping the log, since it gave him a chance to pick up some Black Diamond Rum, available, like ground oatmeal, only in Nova Scotia. The two men, different as different, were like as like, and Han and I loved 'em. We never heard either one speak a good word about the other.

Late on an afternoon tide, one summer well into August, we heard the *Maine* toot, and Han and I ran to be on the wharf when she came up the estuary. Captain Meservey had the wheel and Mate Simmons was ready with a line. The occasion was like the others, but something went wrong and both master and mate lost the tide. The *Maine* sure-enough grounded out and sat aslant all night. The Morning River estuary never drains out completely, so the *Maine* didn't tip all the way, but to be comfortable the two men slept in our houses; the captain at the Marcoux house and Cook Simmons with us. We learned the next day that just before retiring the captain heated his pot of leftover oatmeal, and with molasses and cream had his customary bedtime porridge. He told Mrs. Thomas he couldn't sleep without it. When Mrs. Crowthers heard this the next day, she said, "I always had porridge at bedtime with my father; he came from the Orkneys." This established, Mrs. Crowthers reflected on a way out, and said, "It made me gusty; I had to stop."

The next morning, on the high water, the *Maine* was

properly afloat and would go out to Monhegan Island before tying up to make her two breakfasts. Captain Meservey wouldn't wait to eat with us; he didn't want to lose another tide. So, thinking of everything, perhaps I didn't neglect my education by missing some time with Mr. Thomas, the down-east philosopher.

Chapter 25

CRABMEAT
CAKES

Mrs. Crowthers down-cried fish so often and so uncompromisingly that it was fun later to see her lap up two boiled lobsters when everybody else had one, and there came an evening when she asked why Maine people don't eat more crabmeat. "In Philadelphia," she said, "they make a big thing of crabmeat cakes and consider them a delicacy." Mr. Thomas, always patient with outlander views, told her she had opened a subject with several answers, and he would be happy to devote three to four hours to an impromptu reply. He said Mrs. Thomas made as fine a crabmeat cake as anybody, and all she needed was crabs, which would be provided shortly.

The crab, he said, differs with geography, and the Maine seacoast yields an exceptionally fine crab in texture and in flavor, but he doesn't have so much meat as do others. (Mr. Thomas commenced this dissertation in school-master style, and at this point realized he needed some Monhegan seasoning to sustain interest, and he inserted this:) "Fact is, people claim a man can start picking crabmeat for his own supper, and starve to death before he gets enough."

Han had told me well before this that some day she and I would take the sailing dory and go to an island where we could boil off a hod of crabs and pick and eat them right there. She said crabs were "some old good!" But we hadn't done it—yet.

Mr. Thomas went on: "We get crabs in our lobster traps, and sometimes toss them in a basket to take home. If not, they go overboard with the conchs and starfish and gropies. There's no market for them around here, but I've heard over to the west'ard where crabs have invaded the lobster grounds there are men who fish for crabs and crabmeat factories that buy them. I never heard what they pay.

"Shorty Johnson said he was up-state one time, back along, and a lunchroom had a sign for crabmeat salad sandwiches, and he thought one would taste good and two might be better, so he ordered a couple with a beer and lemon meringue pie, and he looked out through the hole in the wall and watched the man make them. He said the man opened a can of Japanese crabmeat. That's the story. Restaurants won't pay the price for our crabmeat. Around here you don't ask how many sandwiches you get from a crab; you ask how many crabs to a sandwich? But, like anything else you eat, the kind from Maine is always the best, and I'll find some crabs in a few days and Marm'll prove that. You must've heard of the fish plant that got stuck with a load of white salmon and couldn't sell it on the pink salmon market? You didn't? Well, he was originally from Eastport or Lubec, so the fellow packed all the white salmon, and sold it right there in British Columbia. He just pasted on labels that said, 'Guaranteed Not To Turn Pink In The Can.'"

In the summertime, which is off-season for Monhegan lobstering, Mr. Thomas needed some time to find crabs. Word was sent to Rockland where lobster fishermen began keeping crabs for him, and when a bushel was ready it had to be forwarded to Monhegan, and then Cousin Snood brought it to Morning River Farm. Mr. Thomas cooked them off on his clambake fireplace, and then Mrs. Thomas and Han picked out the meat. Cousin Snood showed no haste in returning to Monhegan, so he stayed for flip hour and crabmeat cakes, and he fried the cakes as Mrs. Thomas mixed them batch by batch. Mrs.

Crowthers watched, and Han told her, "It's all so easy when you know how."

After that, at least once every summer, Mrs. Thomas and Mrs. Crowthers combined to make a crabmeat feast, and plans began when Mrs. Crowthers would give an invitation to some passing boat and ask to have it handed to Cousin Snood. Everybody knew Cousin Snood, and he always received the invitation, which said:

MORNING RIVER
CRABCAKE FESTIVAL
Black Tie
Bring Crabs

The date was any date convenient to Cousin Snood. Which meant any date at all.

RECIPE
Mrs. Thomas's Crabmeat Cakes
Assisted by Mrs. Crowthers

> Two brown hen's eggs
> 1/3 cup cow's milk (or equiv.)
> 1-1/3 cup of sifted flour
> two teaspoons cream of tartar
> one teaspoon baking soda
> salt and pepper
> a pint-and-a-half of crabmeat
>   in small pieces

Beat eggs well. Add milk. Add flour sifted with cream of tartar and soda seasoned with salt and pepper. Mix in crabmeat. As for fritters, fry in hot fat until golden brown.

Chapter 26

TO
MONHEGAN
ISLAND

In recollection it seems odd that we were seven summers at Morning River Farm before I went to Monhegan Island. But it was that summer of Han's budding bosom, and without any relevance Mr. Thomas was getting a new boom for his sloop. Cousin Manfred on Monhegan Island was shaping the new boom, and the word came that it was ready. Han had said every summer that we should go to see her house and where she went to school, and everything else, but we'd never done it. So with a clam hod of goodies we set out with Mr. Thomas, and while the boom was being fitted we'd have time to climb the ledge and have our picnic on the top of the island. Mr. Thomas, as usual, took the sloop from our wharf down the estuary, and then Han took the wheel and I was the galley slave who took orders and did the work. I was always smart-aleck about that, and wished all those kids from away, down in Philadelphia, could see me now! Han could shout at me all right, and was ready to at all other times, but when she had the sloop's wheel she spoke softly so I had to listen close, and she always added, "If you please, sir!" I pleased, of course, and Mr. Thomas would look happy that we had listened when he taught. He did tell my father one day that I could handle the sloop as well as he could, and I've always believed Han could handle it even better. Well, that is, if I was crew. Han took us, that day, right to Monhegan Island and laid the sloop to the precise spile where I was to throw a hitch. Mr. Thomas was by no means disappointed that some of his cronies were handy-by to see this demonstration of nautical dexterity. Han was a ham! But then, with an audience I made no false flourishes, either. And we were at Monhegan Island at last!

Mr. Thomas would set us and our lunch ashore, and then go to get his new boom. He didn't know how long it would take, but he'd meet us back here. Han said we wouldn't have time to see everything, but the place to start was "upstairs," and we'd work back down. So I muscled the clam hod and Han led the way, and we began to climb. Han pointed out her house and said her father would pick up a few things her mother wanted. There is a great big "something" about being on Monhegan and perhaps the Island can best be described by an off-islander— me! In the first place, it's awesome to walk along through the magnificent woodland and contemplate that you are hundreds of years ahead of history. Nobody really knows when Europeans first came here, but it was well before anybody discovered it. Can we make-believe that some little fishing boat from Scandinavia or Iberia, it doesn't matter which, got bounced around in an unexpected Fundy Blow, and actually drifted against this foolish rock sticking up from the sea? There is no substitute in this world for chance, and the poor souls on this boat gave thanks to God and went ashore to cut a tree, shape a timber, and make repairs. Going up, they "looked off" and first found out that the Atlantic Ocean was seventy-five times larger than they had expected. On the other side, they first saw the coast of Maine, and had the first dreams of the secret way to far Cathay and the riches of Norumbega and Mattawamkeag. Han and I sat on the peak of "Munhiggin" and leisurely took our sandwiches and cake, and thought about things. There was a definite feeling of height, as if one might roll off, and it was, indeed, a great long way down to the surf on the beach. Captain John Smith was here!

But quite a few years after the Swedes and the Norwegians and the French, and a few Irishmen. When you've been brought up on Columbus, it's hard to be on top of Monhegan Island and realize this is a place he never saw, but he heard about it as a boy when he went from Italy up to Cornwall to get tin. The Cornish people told him, "Yes, we've been getting excellent fish balls from there in recent years." All right, but don't doubt it until you've climbed to the top of Monhegan to see just how close you are to Cornwall! And sit there in admiration until Fairyland has wrought its magic!

There may pass a boat and maybe not. The day Han and I were there a steamer passed on the outside. A tiny toy as in the Christmas pool at Wannamaker's, and Han counted her off at ten knots. "Not quite ten," she said. Han counted seconds with chimpanzeeses. "One chimpanzeeses, two chimpanzeeses, three chimpanzeeses..." Allow fifteen miles to the horizon, but allow for being on top of Monhegan, and you can come pretty close. Han said fishermen seeing a strange light, or hearing a strange foghorn, could count seconds and tell which light and which horn it was. She had an aunt, she said, who could put a cake in the oven and count minutes, second by second, and she never baked a bad cake. Han said she had to do it that way, because she couldn't tell time by a clock. Didn't have a clock anyway. When we were back down off Monhegan, we told Mr. Thomas that we'd watched a steamer go by, and that Han had counted it at not quite ten knots.

Mr. Thomas said, "About on the button. That was the Benson Townes, and the only time she got up to ten knots was with a following wind and being towed. I was engineer on her one summer."

We shared a few sandwich crusts with the gulls, and Han was going to count how many seconds it took a gull to see a crust and get it, but it was less than a chimpanzeeses. So we took a last look in a circle and started down off the top. We hadn't gone far when we came on a bull partridge parading all by himself in great splendor. He had every feather stuck up and looked foolish. He paid no attention to us, but went about ten feet downhill and then came ten feet back. Han said she'd seen him before, and was hoping he'd be here to perform today. His mate, she said, would be near, back in the bushes, and was supposed to be thrilled by his display of affection. But it was late for these mating antics, and the old girl was probably more interested in her chicks. We might see them, Han said, but we didn't. The partridge kept parading, and we walked around him and left him at it.

We hadn't been overlong at our picnic, but Cousins Snood and Manfred had fitted the boom, and the job hadn't taken as long as expected. Mr. Thomas was ready to sail, and we started for Morning River. We didn't get to see Han's school, so left it for "another day." Mr. Thomas already had the things he was to get at the house. Except one thing. He couldn't make out what it was on the list, and Han couldn't read it either. That evening Mrs. Thomas said it was to check that the pantry window was closed. She couldn't remember.

The majesty of the Monhegan peak stayed with me. Time and again in the next few weeks I'd find I'd closed my eyes and could see the ocean. There was a feeling of unsteadiness now and then as I seemed to sense the height and the distance and would teeter. Walking, I'd seem to feel the need of a hand rail and reach for one that wasn't there. When I told Han, she giggled and said it was just the Monhegan afterglow. She said sometimes summer complaints react and have to sit down so they won't fall. "You get over it," she said.

Maybe you do, as a momentary affliction, but the view of God's magnificent world, as seen from the top of Monhegan Island, will stay with you forever.

Chapter 27

LOBSTER BAIT

"Oh," said Han, "you get used to it, and then there's nothing else in all the world half so sweet!" Han was talking about lobster bait, the first time I came to grips with that very loud subject, and she was certainly speaking loyally as a true native of Monhegan Island, where lobster bait has sanctified the scenery for hundreds of boisterous years, and a piquancy prevails that nobody "from away" is ever going to confuse with the word sweet. She was, at the putrid moment, showing me how her father went about compounding the reeking relish he puts in his traps to entice the unwary crustacean into the "bedroom." The bedroom is the compartment in the trap where the lobster arrives to find he can't get out.

Actually, because of the Monhegan fishing season, Mr. Thomas had finished his lobstering before we arrived for the summer from Philadelphia, so technically he wasn't using any of his notorious bait while we were at Morning River Farm. However, he had his storage car for his clam-bake lobsters in the Razor Island Gut, and he had to feed them. His lobster bait was just the thing, so Han and I did what we could to sustain the high quality which kept his captured lobsters healthy and tasty. A wooden tub many years old stood in our shelter on our wharf to contain this nutrient delight, and when needed an adequate dose would be taken in a pail and dumped into the car. Meantime, a tight wooden cover fitted on the tub and was held down by a rock to hold in the vitamins and calories and permit human approach without gastronomic upset. Only those who recall meeting their first bait tub really know. Mainers living within five miles of the tide are used to it. Let me say now that thanks to Han I have, even if I'm from away, got used to it, and when each fall we do go back to Philadelphia it takes me a couple of weeks to realize I'm too far away to get a whiff of Mr. Thomas's superb bait tub.

Every lobsterman, it seems, believes he, and he alone, knows the precise recipe for the bait most favored by the lobsters. Anybody could cry fiddle-faddle at this, but without effect. No minds would change. The basic beginning is some kind of fish well on the way to olfactory intolerance, salted so it will hold its shape long enough to handle. Scraps from a fish packing plant are good, and in season herring, alewives, and pogeys are netted and sold for bait. Every lobsterman has his own ideas about the performance of the various baits. No need to bring in the details here, but some bait is inserted in the trap with a "bait-iron," which is not unlike a chef's larding needle (Mrs. Crowthers uses a larding needle in the kitchen). "Looser" bait is put in a small mesh bag, called a bait bag. Either way, the lobster is attracted by the bait, enters by the "funny-eye" (a funnel eye!) and becomes entrapped and for sale. The bait also attracts other kinds of fish, even cod and haddock, as well as "trash" that gets hove back when the trap is hauled. Altogether too often, the trap will have about everything inside except keeper lobsters.

Han told me her father got a lot of whore's eggs, but he never brought any ashore. Time was, all the fishermen threw them back overboard, but in the past few years there had been a market for them. Living on Monhegan made it impractical to ship them, but lobstermen on the mainland could get them on an evening train for Boston and New York, and whore's eggs made a penny. Han didn't know the right name for whore's eggs, but her father said to call them urchins. They're round shellfish with needles that can prick. Mr. Thomas said the market is Italians and Orientals. One year I had a dried-out shell and I took it home to Philadelphia along with some spruce gum and some Indian arrow points, and I told my teacher, Miss Drayton, that it was a whore's egg. Miss Drayton made me stay after class and we had a talk. She wanted to know where I ever got that, and I said Han told me.

For his food for his lobsters, Mr. Thomas did keep any fish from his traps that was suitable, but not the whore's eggs. He got sculpins, and now and then pollock and even a cod. Starfish and conchs he didn't keep. But Han and I would scull our dory a short ways down the gut and catch a couple of pails of harbor pollock that we'd add to the tub. Then some days we'd catch cunners just for fun and dump them in. Mr. Thomas would take the cover off the tub and look in, sniffing and poking with a finger, to see if we had enough and if it was of dependable quality. "Ah!" he would say, and I could see that Han was right. You get used to it.

Chapter 28

AH!
ROMANCE!

Of Manfred and Snood, cousins to Mr. Thomas, Manfred, with better than average height, good features, and a manly bearing, was the one to be thought of as a lady's man, but it was Cousin Snood, short, fat, and designed like a sausage, who took a shine to Mrs. Crowthers and became what she called her summer romance. She was pleased at this preferment and always had his gingerbread and double flip ready when he showed up at improbable times to woo. Mrs. Crowthers, unbeguiled, always greeted him with, ". . . and how are all the little ones?" This explains our horseshoe pitching rink, or whatever you call it. Snood was a dedicated "shooter" and several times had competed for the state title at some town up in Maine which nobody on Monhegan could locate or pronounce. Mr. Thomas said he believed that one year Cousin Snood had won.

The name Snood bothered me. Everybody else, save we Philadelphians, seemed to know the word Snood and didn't bother to explain, and we Philadelphians didn't inquire. Cousin Snood had shown up for the preparations to lanch our sailing dory, and immediately became my favorite Mainer, and he was already Han's favorite. Were he, in fact, Han's dubious relative, it was ethereal and hypothetical, and Mr. Thomas explained everything by saying Snood's mother was the lighthouse keeper and she left the lamp on all night for callers. Han told me a snood is twine—that is, netting knitted for seining fish, and is also a cap of string worn in the sardine factories so a girl cutting fish won't leak a strand of her hair into a can. Han had no idea why Cousin Snood was called Snood. His head was completely bald. Han said if they didn't call him Snood they'd call him Curly.

One afternoon Han and I had been for our swim, and were drying off in the Croze Nest when Han said there was a boat, and she went to take the cover off the spy-glass, and she said, "It's Cousin Snood!" His boat came up the gut and into our estuary, and by the time Cousin Snood tied up at our wharf Han and I had some clothes on, and we went down to make him welcome. But before we got to the wharf, Mrs. Crowthers had come over from the house and said, "What a pleasant surprise, Mr. Snood! To what are we indebted?" Han and I definitely got the idea she was not at all surprised at his arrival.

Evidently not yet noticing Han and me, Cousin Snood advanced on Mrs. Crowthers to wrap her in his arms and stretch himself into a posture from which he could kiss the lady. They were by no means strangers. Cousin Snood had, indeed, saved her from a watery death back when our sailing dory had been lanched and she, waving the christening bottle, had swung herself overboard. But Mrs. Crowthers wasn't taking that into account, and now outraged at his advances she swung from the ground and caught him full on the chin with a rock-buster. Cousin Snood went limp, and Mrs. Crowthers caught the front of his shirt and lowered him to the wharf gently with comforting concern and soothing words. Han and I could see that Morning River was a-quiver with ardent affection. When Cousin Snood opened his eyes, Mrs. Crowthers said, "Don't you ever try that on me again!" and Cousin Snood said, "Yes, ma'am."

But then they went up to the house for a mug-up, and Cousin Snood stayed for the flip hour, and after that he'd come every so often to pay respects to our cook. That same summer, well before open season, he came with a supply of sea ducks freshly dressed and cut for cooking, and he showed Mrs. Crowthers how to make duck-and-cabbage in the old-time island way. He had a bottle of red wine, used to replace the water that boils away in cooking. We all had duck-and-cabbage for supper at our house, and when Mr. Thomas asked about the ducks, Cousin Snood said he found them in one of his lobster traps that was stored on his piazza. Then another time he came with a set of horseshoes and made Morning River a "shooting" rink. He brought two iron posts and planks to fit around each all cut to size. He measured things off, arranged the planks, and then took our wheelbarrow and went up behind the sawmill to find clay and gravel for the horseshoes to land in. That didn't take long, and then he began teaching Mrs. Crowthers to pitch. He'd show her, and his horseshoe would settle around the iron post for a ringer. Then she'd "shoot," and he'd walk to look in the tall grass and find her shoe. We didn't see Cousin Snood make further advances, and we never knew if she struck him again. It was a decorous courtship, pitched shoe by shoe, and paced by the interminable walking that goes on as the shooters go from stake to stake, over and over again.

Many's the time Han and I would be in the Croze Nest, and suddenly the clang of a steel horseshoe striking the iron stake would invade the silence of Morning River Farm, and we'd look out to see Cousin Snood and Mrs. Crowthers walking back and forth.

Among my souvenirs, so very special that not above a half dozen people have ever seen it, is a lobster shell that Cousin Snood asked me to "keep until I ask it back." The shell is from an extremely big lobster that is very much illegal in Maine. Cousin Snood told me the lobster "went" well over twenty pounds and was delicious. Cousin Snood said it was the biggest lobster he'd ever seen. He said never to show it to anybody who could trace it back to him. Cousin Snood gave me the shell, all wrapped up, as I was leaving for Philadelphia. Han knows about it, but has never seen it. Mrs. Crowthers has never seen it and doesn't know about it. Han and I suspect Cousin Snood doesn't trust her.

Chapter 29

TINKER
MACKEREL

There was one day my father said, "I suppose it would make a difference if they were fresh," and Mrs. Crowthers said, "Not to me it wouldn't, Arruhh!" Then, of course, I went to tell Han. The subject was mackerel. My father had said he didn't care for the mackerel we got in the fish market in Philadelphia, which after great protesting, had been cooked by Mrs. Crowthers, and Mrs. Crowthers had defended her position by saying that mackerel isn't fit to eat anyway and there ought to be a law. Han just said, "Mackerel are good." By that time anything Han said was all right with me, and I was ready to announce that mackerel are good. I had never tasted a mackerel. When Han asked her father he said, "I haven't heard of a mackerel yet, but it's time. I think you'd get some. A few tinkers would go some old good, wouldn't they?"

So Han and I went to jig a few mackerel.

Mr. Thomas said he thought right off the end of Big Razor would be the place to try, and he got us a couple of jigs from the cuddy on his sloop. He said there'd be no need of poles; just let out a couple of fathoms of cunner line with the jig, and if we didn't get a mackerel in ten minutes to wait a few days and they'd start. The breeze was just right to jog a few times in

117

the dory. It took us several minutes to get our dory ready to go. We had to step the mast and set the sail. Han got a couple of water pails, and Mr. Thomas whet a fillet knife for us. "Be careful with it," he said. So we would be down by the end of Razor about at the turn of tide, and as we drifted down the estuary Mr. Thomas called, "Get some tinkers, never mind the whoppers!" Han told me little mackerel are called spikes, and then come tinkers. Tinkers make the best eating.

I asked Han what makes the best mackerel bait, and she said, "Don't trail your finger overboard!" She showed me the jigs her father had given us. They were a piece of bright metal with a hook and an eye for the fishline. The mackerel struck at the bright metal. Han said, "A piece of white cloth is good. Anything is mackerel bait." While we were going down the gut Han tied the two jigs onto two lengths of line, and we were all ready to start fishing when the dory swung around. "Let it drag," said Han. Almost at once something attracted my attention, and Han said, matter of fact like, "One's on!" I had a mackerel. And then Han had one. "Take the sail!" she said, and she pulled in my fish, slapped it against a thwart so it came off the hook and fell in a bucket, and then she pulled in her mackerel. I'm here to state, as a willing witness right out of Philadelphia, that there is nothing more than that to fishing for mackerel down east in Maine.

When I threw my jig back in the water to get a second mackerel, dozens of fish came up to make a great swirl by the jig, and I had my second fish. Han had shown me how, and I was on my own. "Bang him in the bucket!" she said, and she brought in her second mackerel. We didn't turn the dory about for a second pass; we had enough, and Han said they were just tinker size and her father would be glad.

Han said it was better to use just one jig and take one at a time, but that some liked five or six hooks spaced maybe two feet apart. You'd get five or six fish at once, but the line would tangle on you and you could get a hook where you didn't want a hook. Han said we had mackerel enough, and we'd dress them back at the wharf. She wanted to show me how to do that, because mackerel have their own way. We hadn't been gone long enough to matter and when he saw us coming, Mr. Thomas thought we'd been skunked. He was at the wharf when the dory came in next to his sloop.

"Too early?" he asked, and then he saw our pail of fish. He got his own knife out while we were tying up, and reached for the pail. Han said, "You told me always to gut my own fish!" He said, "Right! I'll just help."

So Han and her father, both, showed me how to clean a mackerel, and that was one of my best recollections of all my summers at Morning River Farm. Maybe there are people who would just as soon not get involved in gutting fish. But it, too, has its art and its skills. A mackerel is not opened from the belly as are other fish, but from the back, leaving the meat to be filleted handily and with the bones going into the gurrybutt. Mr. Thomas, between Han and me at our cutting board, said, "I think from what your father said he got some mackerel that was dressed by a handicapped highlander! Now, you watch here!"

With the blade of his knife he pointed at the brown strips along the mackerel's white sides, and he said, "This is oily and full of small bones, and it's best to emasculate it, if I may coin a phrase." With his knife he simply cut away the brown strips and threw them off the wharf into the water. "Pleases the eels too," he said. Han was doing the same, and then they made me do it. If Philadelphia ever needs a mackerel dresser, I'm your man! While we were finishing the pail of mackerel, Mr. Thomas told me, "I mistrust your father got some city mackerel that lacked competent surgery! We'll try these on him and listen to him yell for more!"

I said, "Maybe Mrs. Crowthers?" Mr. Thomas said, "That's a thought; I'll have a word with her, too."

Our dory was messy with mackerel scales, so it took a while to wash things down. At the Marcoux house Mrs. Thomas said, "I thought I'd fry, but wouldn't it be nice to grill these?" So Mr. Thomas got some charcoal from the sawmill and lit it in his picnic fireplace at the shore, and during flip hour he trotted back and forth to attend his mackerel, our mackerel, and Mrs. Crowthers said she'd try a mackerel but she knew she wouldn't like it. At least, though, if we were all going to eat at the Marcoux house tonight, she wouldn't have to make supper. Perhaps, she said, I could have another flip?

Chapter 30

OUR SMOKEHOUSE

After my father had run out the string on his salt fish "business," either the next summer or the next, Han and I found the remains of the old smokehouse. It was in the side of the hill by the cascade, and since it hadn't been used in long years it had weathered. We found it while looking for a woodchuck hole. We saw the woodchuck, sitting on his hind legs, and Han said his hole in the ground was probably right beside where he was sitting and when we got there we found some boards that covered a hole in the ground which was certainly not that of any woodchuck. Han surmised what it was and we went to tell my father. He said he guessed we were right, and to wait until Mr. Thomas came back. Mr. Thomas walked up with us and said yes, it was the old smokehouse. There was a place to build a fire, then a tile to let the smoke go up into the smoking cave. The whole thing had been stoned up, but without mortar, so winters and summers had done their damage. It would take more than a little work to get the thing ready to smoke again. Mr. Thomas said he didn't know much about a smokehouse, but his cousin Snood still had one that worked and maybe he'd come some day. He'd ask him.

In about two weeks, Cousin Snood came and said he'd

need a day to dig away loose dirt, replace stones, and arrange a tight cave with a rig that would hold in the smoke. Then he told Han and me to get a clam hod full of green bush juniper tips, some green alder—five or six good-sized pieces—and he'd bring a bag of dry corncobs. He had corncobs laid away. And, he said, we can smoke some trout for a starter. He said, "You can't beat a smoked trout for some old goo-ood!"

As he had with the beached up hake, my father now became interested in reviving an other old custom. Mr. Thomas told him, and Han and me, that green alder, juniper, and corn cobs were the traditional rules for smokehouse smoke and were good for hams and bacons, as well as any jerky and fish. He said the early Morning River people probably smoked a lot of salmon and trout, lots of alewives, and probably deer meat and birds. He said to wait and he'd let Cousin Snood answer my father's questions.

So Cousin Snood came and fixed our smokehouse and had a trial fire, and said he'd let us know when he'd come to smoke, and he'd give Han and me at least two days' notice so we could get a mess of trout.

Which he did, and when Mr. Thomas came back from Monhegan with Cousin Snood's message, he had a short piece of stick that showed the size of the trout Han and I were to get for smoking. No longer and no shorter—all the same. And to leave the heads on when we dressed them. That would give him the gills so he could hang them on a stick the way he did alewives. By that time Han and I, and my father, were all heifered up over the smokehouse, and Han and I went the next day to get the trout. Cousin Snood had sent word that we could get any amount—the smokehouse was big enough.

The little stick Cousin Snood had sent was just eleven inches long. Larger or smaller, Han and I tossed them back. When we had two dozen we dressed them and pulled moss to line our baskets. A trout that size will weigh right around a pound, so we each had some twelve pounds to carry home. It was cool that evening, so we left the trout in the wet moss right in the baskets, but we set the baskets in our Croze Nest so raccoons wouldn't bankrupt us. Cousin Snood arrived in his boat before Mr. Thomas left for the day, and had a mug-up with us. He raved over the twenty-four matched brook trout. "A picture no artist can paint!" he kept saying, and I could see the tell-tale spots of the true eastern brook trout did have something other fish lack. Then, too, twenty-four of them arranged on our green moss was a spectacular sight. Cousin Snood said it was like a sunset; before an artist could get his brush in position the color would change.

Cousin Snood took his dishes to the sink, thanked Mrs. Crowthers for the mug-up, and said it would take at least two days to get a smoke on that mess of trout and he'd show us how to do things and then leave it for us to finish. Not my father; Han and me. He sounded as if he didn't trust my father one little bit!

Cousin Snood had some small pieces of dry hardwood, and he kindled them in a round metal pan that showed it had been used this way many times. In a minute or so he put the pan in the lower cave of the smokehouse, on a flat rock, and got it in the right position before it got too hot. Then more dry wood, and he waited until things were ready to subside into embers. He kept explaining everything to me and Han. Now he laid on some green alder, and on top of that some corn cobs. Things began to smoke when he covered the pan with juniper tips. These were ground juniper, and with the gin berries.

And didn't things smoke! Cousin Snood told us the pan would send up smoke for several hours, and he positioned the boards that closed the entrance. The smoke would pass up through the tile into the upper cave, where the trout were on long sticks, head to head, hanging like clothes in a closet. Lacking a draft, the pan wouldn't flare up, but would just smudge along and make smoke. The trout would hang in the smoke and be cured. When the smudge had cooled down and the smoke had thinned, Han and I were to start another fire just as he had, and now he was going home. Han and I could start a third fire at breakfast time if we were up and around before he came, but he'd be back in the morning to see how the smoke was doing. He thought a third good smoke might be enough. Mrs. Crowthers had some gingerbread hot from the oven, and Cousin Snood went out the estuary just as Mr. Thomas was coming in from one of his clam bakes. Han and I cleaned up the sloop and left her for the night, and then jumped in the millrace pool. We probably smelled that way too, but we certainly felt smoky. Our eyes stung from the juniper tips.

Although Cousin Snood came early, Han and I had a new smoke going already. Snood saw that it was a good smoke and that we had closed any draft, and then he had his mug-up with Mrs. Crowthers and my mother and father. He and my father discussed all phases of smoking meats, the different kinds of smokes, and how to make a sugar-salt brine for hams, bacon, and shoulders. Also, he said to finish off a ham, put some sumac "tossels" to smoke for the last couple of hours. "Gives it class," he said. My father said he doubted if he'd ever raise a pig, and Cousin Snood said, "If you do, get me to smoke it! I'm the best!"

This was late in our summer, so we gave Cousin Snood what he'd take of our trout, Mr. and Mrs. Thomas, and Han, took a supply to the island, and we wrapped the rest for a trip to Philadelphia. Nobody, anywhere, found fault; even Mrs. Crowthers granted that smoked trout was sheer delight. "Of course," she said, "fish is one thing, and trout's another. We have to grant that." When the sloop was ready and we ended our summer and started back for Philadelphia, Han and I said goodbye and agreed we'd start next summer, next June, with another trout smoke. She'd make sure Cousin Snood had the smokehouse ready.

And Mrs. Crowthers promised gingerbread.

Chapter 31

LOOKING FOR BINGHAM LAND

After Mr. Thomas explained why my father's taxes on the Morning River property are paid at the Maine statehouse in Augusta, my father started buying up surrounding land to create a "buffer." He hoped to prevent an influx of folks from away who could "organize" and out-vote us, thus changing the whole character of our Garden of Eden. He did acquire the land, but I suppose none of us will be around in three hundred years to see what has really happened. So be it, but my father brought together a group of real estate agents who helped him, and they called themselves the William Bingham Land Associates. It was a dummy company with my father in control and with his Winnifred down in Philadelphia doing his work, if any. These associates were all in the real estate business in their own communities and everybody, except my father and Winnifred, were registered agents and brokers.

My father first heard of William Bingham when he came to Maine looking for lapsed trackage rights the Pennsylvania Railroad might like to acquire. Every time he looked up a land title, it seemed, it went back to one William Bingham. He asked a few people in the registries about William Bingham, and got some fuzzy answers. Everyone knew there had been a William

Bingham, and that he was a big landowner, and that was that.

And when he came to buy the Morning River land, he wondered if he was about to find that William Bingham had owned that. He hadn't. The title to Morning River went back beyond the days of William Bingham, and in two separate deeds was conveyed to Jabez Knight. One by the English Crown and again by the French. Later, both those deeds, or grants, were confirmed by both governments, as of New England and as of New France, and then went on record again as Jabez split the farm down the middle and gave Jules Marcoux a life-time half interest. There was more at the county registry at Wiscasset, so Morning River Farm lacked no proof of title, and William Bingham never had anything to do with the place. Jabez Knight was there first.

My father was disappointed because he had hoped to find Bingham somewhere in his title. At one time William Bingham had owned just about a tenth part of the District of Maine. He, too, was a Philadelphian and was probably considered to be from away. He was politically active in the preliminaries to the American Revolution, and being wealthy he helped finance the war. He had been in the Continental Congress, and after the war was over he served Pennsylvania in the United States Senate. When land in the Massachusetts District of Maine was offered, he bought heavily. His "Kennebec Purchase" became known as the Three Million Acre purchase, and his Penobscot Purchase in eastern Maine was even larger. He did visit Maine once, in black fly time of 1796, and wrote a description of his holdings. He died in England in 1804. My father had William Bingham looked up, and read what the Philadelphia Public Library had about him. I remember most of one winter we got William Bingham every evening at supper, and my father was disappointed that he couldn't brag about having a little Bingham land.

It was his blessed Winnifred that resolved this in her customary manner of making difficult things easy. "Why don't you quit harping on his Bingham, and I'll get you the three million acres he did own?"

In a few days, a round-robin went to all the William Bingham Land Associates in Maine to look for something once owned by William Bingham.

Winnifred became William Bingham, although to my father and the others in the office it stopped at "Billy Bing." She was empowered to use the name for business purposes, and signed his name when needed with a grand flourish that John Hancock never quite had.

A little time passed, and the associate in the town of, appropriately, Bingham wrote that a considerable parcel of stripped woodland was expected to go on the market shortly, including Mount Hunger and Mayfield Plantation. The lot was the site of the abandoned Mayfield slate quarry.

Billy Bing told my father, and he liked the idea. He not only wanted to be able to say he owned some Bingham land, but he was much taken with the thought of owning a slate quarry, even though the associate had explained that the deposit of slate had run out and what was left was a deep hole in the mountain filled with stagnant water and seams of slate with no market value. Winnifred told the associate in Bingham to get an option to buy when the lot was placed on sale.

I remember that during the rest of that winter we heard less about Landowner William Bingham of Philadelphia, and quite a bit about mining slate and the manufacture of slate shingles and billiard tables. Billy Bing would go to the library and get the books.

Chapter 32

WE BUY
RAZOR LAND

The first land my father acquired in his desire to own a "buffer" around his Morning River property, and thus frustrate people "from away" who might move in and organize a town, forever spoiling our little paradise in Maine, was Big Razor Island. Everybody in a hundred miles declared he was crazy. Even though Little Razor Island came too at no extra price, he was still crazy. Mr. Thomas, much amused at this purchase, said, "Well, from now out, there's no way to do except better!" The Razor Islands, ledges and wind, are not choice property.

Big Razor Island was across the Razor Island Gut from our place. A gut, in Maine talk, is a narrow strip of tidewater. It was deep enough in Razor Island Gut for vessels of some size, but if a skipper wasn't acquainted with the waters he'd go out around the island on the ocean side. Little Razor, included in the deal, was no more than the backbone of a ledge, covered at a high tide. Nobody ever owned the Razors and nobody ever lived there until Manny the Portygee came in the days of Jabez Knight and used it as a base for his several enterprises. Manny was a pirate, and so forth. He had a beautiful schooner, jackass rigged, and made so many voyages a year to the West Indies, also going east around Nova Scotia to the Madeleines. He was a Portuguese nobleman, registered with the Port Authority in Boston as Dom Affonso Manuel Henriques Alferes Mor Do Póvoa Varzim entre Minho e Doura. Mr. Thomas said children in the Monhegan Island school memorized his name and used it as a rhyme to skip jump rope. He had inherited vineyards in the Apporto Valley, but had never gone to claim his rights.

Manny became a valued friend of the Morning River folks, and sometimes helped in the sawmill, taking a few boards now and then instead of wages. In this way he got lumber and built a small house on Big Razor Island—the only dwelling ever there. Manny's house had a glass tower, but it wasn't a lighthouse. By the time my father bought the Razor Islands Manny's house had tumbled in, or more likely had blown down. Han and I went over to the island now and then, but never found more than a few old boards.

There was never anything on Little Razor except sunning seals, but Big Razor did have spruce trees. At the far end from us, east, a stand of spruce made a place for Great Blue Herons to nest, and ducks hatched under those trees on the ground. Also, sea gulls nested on the ledges. There was a cove, entered from the ocean side, where Manny would moor his schooner in heavier winds, but sometimes that wasn't harborage enough, and he'd bring his schooner around into our gut and moor her in the lee. Razor Island did protect us at Morning River from the onshore winds that plagued Manny. But Manny wasn't too often at home. He had a flag he'd run up on a pole when he was there, and the folks at Morning River also had a flag to run up if they wanted to see Manny. Manny was said to be a smuggler and pirate and maybe even worse, but nobody ever seemed to be sure of this as a fact. Mr. Thomas said Manny was greatly admired by everybody who had anything to do with him in his time, esteemed and respected. At one time he tried to buy the Razor Islands.

Mr. Thomas enlivened a couple of flip hours with his account of this transaction, as he had heard it from tradition and, presumably, had bettered it with native talent. Manny's principal partner in smuggling was a defrocked Catholic priest on the Madeleine Islands, who arranged contraband shipments and then Manny came with his schooner to deliver and collect. Since Manny lacked English, he sailed to the Madeleines and brought Father Hermidore to Razor Island, and then to Wiscasset where they found a lawyer to arrange for Manny to buy the Razor Islands. The interview with this lawyer was attempted in English, French, and Portuguese with incredulous success, and Mr. Thomas explained that it didn't take much in those days to buy some Maine Islands. Manny then took Father Hermidore back to the Madeleines and in due time would get his deed from the statehouse.

Mr. Thomas said that Manny was what Maine fishermen call "lucky." The frequently heard expression is, "lucky as a dog with an extra penis." Everything Manny did proved successful and fortunate. He had signed an agreement to pay for the Razor Islands, but he hadn't paid yet. He bided at the Madeleines a few days to conclude some transactions with Father Hermidore and to enjoy his pious company, and without incident came home to find his mooring cove was full of mackerel. Nobody had ever seen any mackerel in that cove, and nobody remembered any old-time talk about there ever being any. As Manny sailed in he noticed disturbed waters, as if something was schooling, and when he saw it was mackerel he broke out a seine stored under a dory on deck, and he stopped the entrance to the cove in an adroit manner common with old hands along the Maine coast, previous to which he moved his schooner out into the sea. He left the dory in the cove.

Now Manny directed the course of his schooner a bit east of south, a matter of about two miles, where he knew a pogey boat was anchored for the summer.

This was part of Manny's luck. The pogey is known in college as the menhaden, and is an oily fish not admired for lunch. It schools in great numbers and can be netted fairly easily by the tens of thousands. In those times, said Mr. Thomas, a pogey boat would stay in one place during pogey season, and fishermen would bring netted pogeys from which the bountiful fish oil would be extracted for various industrial uses. The pogey boat was a factory. Even the residue, after the oil was removed, could be used. Almost all paint, then, had pogey oil in it. Manny, now, interrupted the pogey oil business and directed all the fishermen to Razor Island, where a coveful of mackerel awaited them with promise of profit much greater than pogeys could offer. It would take at least three days to clean out the cove. Most of the mackerel went to Portland, but some to Rockland and Bath. Mr. Thomas said the financing was simple and easy. Manny drew on his bank in Brussels for sufficient money, and the manager on the pogey-oil boat paid the tariff to the fishermen who took mackerel from the cove. Then the buyers at the fish markets deposited what they owed Manny as per instructions, a small percentage to the pogey manager for his kindness. Seventy-eight thousand bushels of mackerel run into money, and Manny hadn't even paid for Razor Island yet.

Manny never did pay for it. About two weeks later, and before the State of Maine got around to drawing him a deed, the slave girl came into the picture.

She was an African some sea captain had picked up, and somehow she was given to Elzada. There was nothing illegal about slaves in Maine then but nobody kept any, and Elzada planned to give the girl her freedom as soon as she could find out how this should be done properly. So Manny took the young lady to the Madeleine Islands, where Father Hermidore made them man and wife, and with the money from his mackerel in several chests he sailed his schooner with bride back to the Valley of the Apporto River, where his domain was waiting his attention.

Mr. Thomas said, "Isn't that a good story? And never again has anybody seen a mackerel in Manny's cove!"

The State of Maine never had another chance to sell the Razor Islands until my father made his approach. There were records about Manny's attempt to buy, but nobody could find the paper on which he agreed to pay when he got a deed. Possibly nobody owned Razor Island. My father searched in several counties, and decided the Razor Islands were in the public domain, and if he could get any kind of a deed it would be good. He made an offer of ten dollars, which Manny was said to have agreed to pay so many long years ago, but the state clerk handling such things said that was just ridiculous. He said the seaweed was worth that. How about twice that?

So for twenty dollars we had a start on securing the future of Morning River. My father is spending something like two hundred dollars for a bronze tablet to be fastened to the ledge where Manny kept his boat. It says, "MANNY'S COVE." My father says that all Maine folks such as Manny the Portygee should be remembered forever by a grateful people.

Chapter 33

MEDITATIONS

It was several years after my growing up that I fell to thinking how Han and I ran around in our skin and nobody seemed to care. Everybody knew about that, but it didn't take many people to make "everybody" at Morning River. And it's true that Han and I never thought about it unless some adult caused us to. Mr. Thomas said a couple of things about bathing suits, and then Mrs. Thomas told me to be a good boy. My father attempted a talk with me but failed to make much progress, and at the time I didn't know what he was trying to say. And I think my mother chose to avoid the subject.

Anyway, after a summer in Maine we came back to Philadelphia and I resumed my haphazard studies at Sunday School, and we started at the beginning with the Creation. I think I was properly justified in my attitude. Well, here's a pious young man unversed in the lingo of sin, and as far as he knows it's perfectly correct for a boy and a girl to undress and go swimming. Now this young man is in Sunday School down in Philadelphia, and a very much embarrassed Miss Sidney is telling him that Adam and Eve were greatly disturbed because they were naked. Miss Sidney used naked as a Sunday School teachers' dirty word, and all she did was set the young man to thinking how much he missed Han. Why would Adam and Eve be ashamed? It didn't make sense to me. How did they know they were naked? Who was around to be telling such things to the first man and the first woman? I drifted into my own thoughts while Miss Sidney, blushing, dwelt on naked shame, and I wondered what Han would say about this. Then I had to choke back a laugh, which would have bothered Miss Sidney at that moment, because I could hear Han saying, "Twarn't shame at all made 'em go for clothes. It was Maine winter comin' on!"

My mother chose to avoid the matter, probably because Mrs. Crowthers had given me my bath since I was born, and was no stranger to my bare backside. Han and I were eight when we first stripped for a swim, and even then if I showed up at table with grimy elbows, Mrs. Crowthers would waltz me to her kitchen and clean me at the sink with laundry soap and a rough towel. I remember Mr. Thomas made a couple of pointed remarks about bathing suits, but otherwise made no effort to inform me and Han that it was socially tacky to go without. Mrs. Thomas certainly didn't have bathing suits in mind when she told me to be a good boy. For that matter, years later my mother told me what Mrs. Crowthers had said in the kitchen when she first heard that Han and I didn't wear bathing suits. My mother said Mrs. Crowthers brought her clasped hands up to her chin in a gesture of approval, and said, "Oh! The sweet little angels!"

Accordingly, there was no way I should feel ashamed before God because I didn't have my pants on, and while Miss Sidney continued to stammer and stutter about Adam and Eve, and she and Moses were dressing them for Christian decency, in my reveries Han was dressing them because it was fall on Monhegan Island and the bird bath had ice every morning.

I tell you this: When, in my grown-up reveries I think of Han as I do, I think of her not in shame in the millrace pool. Not at all, never. My clearest recollection of Han is of the day she swat the two-run homer at the Strawberry Festival. The team shirt she was wearing was large for her and it flopped as she rounded the bases, her pigtail with an elastic band straight out backwards. That's my best picture of Han. When she stepped on third she knew the ball was over the fence, so she slowed and straightened her shirt.

I read the letters on the shirt:

```
         N
      I     B
    A         O
   R           W
       GIRLS
```

Chapter 34

OUR DAY
ON RAZOR

The day of our great lanch when we put the sailing dory of Master Builder Jabez Knight back in the water was one of the best in our Morning River memories, but equally good, although less sociable and without big hooraw, was the day Han and I were permitted to take the dory all by ourselves and visit Big Razor Island. Han and I did all right, but Mr. Thomas gave us a good scare. Those two days did not come close together. Han and I spent a great many days between, getting ready to sail a dory under stern discipline by Mr. Thomas.

All Maine fisherman, I decided early, and all coastal Mainers, live in fear that one day the ocean is going to sneak up on them, and in some unexpected way will deal a fearful blow. Mr. Thomas was typical about this and had brought Han up so she was not impatient with his constant drilling. Now he had me to teach, and he started again from the beginning, giving Han at the same time a complete review. It seemed to me there was no way I could please him. Every time he'd show me how to make a knot, I'd have to pull on it and yank again, and then he would give it a jerk, and if it slipped in the slightest way I'd be told what caused it to slip, and what I'd done wrong, and I tied it over again until it didn't slip. "Some day," Mr. Tho-

mas said, "you'll be some glad that thing don't slip on you!"
Now and then he'd say to Han, "Show him how you do that,"
and this wasn't always to instruct me, but for Han to show that
she remembered and wasn't about, ever, to forget.

So we'd sail up and down the Razor Island Gut, doing
things over and over, and patiently, even tediously, getting ready
to suit Mr. Thomas enough to get his permission to "go two"
on our own. Not many people frequented the gut so we were
watched, but a few did, and we always got the same comment:
"She's pretty!" I think they were really admiring the craftsmanship of Jabez Night, rather than the dory herself, because a dory
is not really a thing of grace and charm. Built for work, she is
rightly rowed, and the oars for a dory are long and hard to work
and are known as sweeps. Built for hand lining and trawl fishing on the Banks, dories were "nested" on the deck of a fishing
schooner, and lowered one at a time when the schooner was
"over the grounds." The two men in each were "dorymates,"
and each relied on the other absolutely against that unexpected
thrust of the ocean about which Mr. Thomas was so seriously
preparing Han and me. Dorymates were even closer than brothers. The dory was the "safest" boat afloat, and anything at all
frivolous was left out. She was never meant to have a sail, and
being flat on her bottom she'd go sideways if one was rigged.
When, for reasons of sparing the sweeps, somebody fitted a sail,
the only feasible kind was a small "sprits'l" set well forward on
a slim mast that was stepped only when the sail was in use. By
a stick held in his hand, the sailor manipulated the sprits'l both
to catch wind and to steer the boat. Cousin Snood showed up
several times while Han and I were being trained by Mr. Thomas, and mostly he kept repeating what Mr. Thomas said about
knots that slipped and being always ready for disaster. If it will
ease anybody's mind, Han and I never had the slightest suggestion of ill-luck with our sailing dory, and we used it a lot. I don't
mean to say that the ocean eased off on us; I'll leave it that Mr.
Thomas, and Cousin Snood, were exacting teachers. They
wanted us to be just as scairt of that ocean as they were.

The day came when Mr. Thomas said he thought we were ready, but he wanted to see us swim. He'd promised my father that he'd make sure about that. "I don't mean in a swimming pool, or in that sun-bath up by the sawmill," he said. "I mean out there when the tide's running and where a polar bear gives up in two minutes. I want to see that you can fall out and get back aboard."

So he had the stick to the sprits'l, and he said, "Now!" Han and I kicked off our shoes and dropped our clothes, and over we went. It was some colder than up in the spillway water, but not too much, and we swam around the dory a couple of times and then came aboard by the stern. Mr. Thomas said, "Where are your bathing suits?" Han said, "We don't wear any."

Han said her father and her mother had a talk about this during that evening, but they didn't say anything to her. Han figured maybe they thought it was already late in the game. And that concluded our training and our examination about using the sailing dory, and from then on Han and I were permitted to use it as we pleased. And we were plenty proud and excited the morning we went out to spend a day on Outer Razor, mug-up and all, and the little digging tools Cousin Snood made for us so we could hunt in the shellheap for Indian arrow points.

Mr. Thomas drew us a course marking the shellheap and a place to have a fire, which was at "Manny's Cove," and he said he'd come by with his sloop in the afternoon to see that we got started home all right. He said we would probably get a fresh westerly and it was well to be sure. If the day of the lanch was outstanding, this was its equal.

And don't anybody think we didn't all know that! Mrs. Crowthers was truly in a "dither." She worried that we might have to spend the night and would run out of food. She said we weren't big enough to overturn the dory and make a shelter. She said it might come up a storm. My father said, "I don't have one single thing in my boyhood to match this!" My mother said, "Then be glad the gods favor you to make it available now." Mr. Thomas said, "Be sure the painter's made to a good tree!" And

Cousin Snood, who came in from the island for such an important occasion, called, "You got matches?" Then Cousin Snood gave our dory a push and made believe lose his balance so he had to grab Mrs. Crowthers.

To me, Han said, "Want to take her?"

I said, "No. Not now. We've got a long day."

And Han said, "Hope somebody wants permission to come aboard." She made her point. She was captain and I was crew. Our boat, all the way. We had drifted from the wharf and the estuary into the gut, and Han moved the stick so the sail picked up a breath of wind, and we were under sail. We would go westerly and around the end of the island, then easterly on the seaward side until we came to the sandy beach and then the inlet to Manny's Cove. Along the way we hoped to find a mackerel to fry for our lunch, and at the sandy beach was a safe place to have a fire. We had only to put in our time. I got a bucket ready and Han tossed me a wound-up line with a mackerel jig on it. We were ripping right along now at a snail's pace. The sailing dory is not famous for great haste. There is always a swell and surf on Outer Razor, so we had some bumps, but not bad, and I did get a mackerel almost at once, so we paid attention to fishing instead of the water. I got four and that was more than we'd eat. I dressed them and laid them in the pail, and I rubbed some gurry on the thwart so Han could see it. We now had an experienced dory! And, we'd have to wash things down when we went ashore. Mr. Thomas would look to see if we had.

Then a raven came out of the spruce woods, and surprised by our boat he let loose a dubious croak before he turned on one wing and flew back into the spruces. We looked for a nest but saw none. A raven is a big crow and always looks bigger than that, and this one was even bigger. Then, as if maybe we and the raven had disturbed them, an eider duck with her clutch came bursting in one big quack out of the spruces and went over our heads and off to at least Monhegan Island. Han sat there holding the little stick on the sprits'l composed and unruffled, and I, facing her, liked what I saw and had a thought that perplexes me still, after so many years. I just happened to think, as if I were then much-much older, "Han and I are ten years old."

Foreseeing a fish fry, Mother Thomas had sent some cold boiled potatoes for us to fry, and some seasoned butter for both the potatoes and our fish. The fire we started with driftwood was too big to cook on, so we had a swim while it went to embers. We poured water from the Grand Bank carboy in the dory for a pot of tea, and we fixed stones to support our cold biscuits while they toasted. Manny's Cove was comfortable for a swim, and as the tide was still coming we had no worries that our dory would beach out. Han said we'd have a good three hours.

Han had brought the dory into the mouth of the cove as if she'd been docking sailing dories the past fifty years, and as I caught the bow so it wouldn't run up on the sand she hopped ashore and said, "I'll let you take her home."

Han found some hen clams on the cove shore. These are a different breed and are huge. Sometimes they're called surf clams. Han shucked them and quartered them, and we fried them in some of the seasoned butter. At last we heated some water from the carboy and rinsed our dishes and pans, and if we had been marooned by one of Mrs. Crowthers' catastrophes, we would indeed have been without food.

When we got to it, we looked for some Indian relics, but found only a few flakes of flint. That showed, though, that we were somewhat in the right place, and we took note with plans to return another time. It was said some good relics had been found on Razor Island by others. We did decide that the little tools Cousin Snood had made were just right.

We'd kept an eye on our dory so it wouldn't beach out on us, and when we guessed the time was right we started back. I did handle the sprits'l, and Lucky Me, I caught a good snort right away, and almost at once the same raven came out and croaked at us and we knew we were homeward bound. Han said we should be seeing her father's sloop before too long.

It has fascinated me to see two sailboats, both using the

same wind, meet and pass head on, one coming and one going, and before I saw Mr. Thomas handling his sloop I didn't know how they arranged that. So now, heading westerly in our sailing dory, I fell to thinking about meeting Mr. Thomas, coming easterly in his sloop, and rehearsing in my mind the maneuvers I must use to suit nautical courtesies. But when we sighted a boat, she was not a sloop. Han recognized the power lobster boat and she said, "It's Cousin Snood with Cousin Manfred!" The boat came to us in no time and slowed, and I spilled the wind. It was Manfred and Snood, and Manfred said to Snood, "It's Han, his daughter!"

Snood said, "Good Jesus!"

Manfred tried to be tactful. He said, "Han, we're looking for your daddy." Han didn't connect, so she said, "He'll be along; he's about to meet us at the end of Razor Island."

"Eyah," said Manfred. "We know." He looked at Snood. Snood said, "Suthin's happened, Han. We found his sloop." Manfred said, "Adrift!"

I had connected. Something had happened and they were looking for Mr. Thomas. And now Han had connected. She smiled. "He'll turn up," she said. "Where's his sloop?" The sloop had been found adrift and been towed to Morning River. When Mr. Thomas wasn't at Morning River, the hunt began. Cousin Snood asked, "Can you two get back all right? We can tow you around."

Han said, "Look some more; he's not east of here. He'll turn up." Cousin Manfred put his power in gear, but I twisted my stick and our dory was moving before his lobsterboat was. He turned in a wide jogging circle around us and was soon out of hearing and out of sight. Han had no doubts about her father. "He'll turn up," she had said, and now as Manfred and Snood were gone Mr. Thomas, himself, called from the island shore, "Ahoy!"

Mr. Thomas was in his underwear, but he was all right. Let us say he was physically all right. But he was miserably embarrassed. After he called ahoy and had our attention he stepped behind a tree to get his shirt and pants, and they dripped as he laid them over his arm. He splashed out the few feet to our dory and climbed aboard, tossing his pants and shirt on a thwart and then sitting on them. He was shivering. Mr. Thomas said, "I warn't about to let Snood and Manfred see me in my underwear! Did they find the sloop?"

Han said, "She's tied up at Morning River. Just a-drift, is all."

"Eyah," said Mr. Thomas. When we got to Morning River my father hurried Mr. Thomas to the house and got a good shot of whiskey into him, and then trotted him around the property until he stopped shivering. That dreaded and unexpected misfortune that was one day to leap up had at last come to the Mr. Thomas on the list of names. Having rounded Razor Island, Mr. Thomas was sailing along happily, expecting every moment to encounter two youngsters in a sailing dory, and a bluebill duck had plopped from the sky into the sloop and had knocked himself out. Reaching to learn if this duck was sufficiently expired to be skun out for the pot, Mr. Thomas was answered by a great flapping of wings in his face and eyes, and in the illusion that Pemaquid Lighthouse had fallen on the sloop, Mr. Thomas waded ashore, falling down several times, and had just taken off some of his wet clothes when he saw Snood and Manfred approaching. So the sea didn't get Mr. Thomas, and shortly Mrs. Crowthers was askin' Han and me if we'd had a good day.

Chapter 35

SEA
LAVENDER

The summer Han and I went into the flower business kept us so busy we never did that again. I remember exactly how it started. Mrs. Thomas said, "It's August!" And it was right after breakfast on the first day of August—the last month of summer before we jokers from away started home to Philadelphia. Mrs. Thomas said to Han, "Get some cankerwort soon's-it's ready to take to M'nhiggin. They got plenty off there, but everybody always forgets to gather any. I like to see a bottle full of it on the teacher's desk." So that was something else Han could explain to me.

August was cankerwort time, but it would be a couple of weeks yet and we'd find plenty right down at the shore. Over across the gut it grew all the way around Razor Island. The old folks used to boil it and keep the water for a mouth rinse—supposed to cure cankers and mouth sores. Sea lavender was a nicer name. It dried and would keep on a mantle piece all winter without water.

So Han kept one eye looking for sea lavender, and one morning gave me a fillet knife and a clam hod, and we walked down to the shore to pick flowers—the sweetest and dearest little

angel-star flower I know anything about. Razor Island may well
be surrounded by sea lavender, but Han and I never went to find
out. We could pick all we needed right on our own shore. It
grew along the high tide mark, a small clump of a plant, with
stiff stems a foot and more tall, with a spray of small blossoms
in a lavender persuasion. We got enough so both our houses
had table bouquets, and Mrs. Thomas had plenty to go to the
island.

Han took a bunch to the big house and gave it to Mrs.
Crowthers. Mrs. Crowthers looked at it, held it to her face, and
said, "Where'd you find that?"

Han said, "Down to the sho-wer. You don't have to hunt
for it. There's miles of it."

"That's sea lavender," said Mrs. Crowthers. "Do you
have any idea what a flower shop in Philadelphia gets for a
bunch that size?" We had nothing to do with it. Mrs. Crowthers
took over and set us up in a very profitable mail order business.
She took a bouquet of sea lavender back to Philadelphia, and
that next winter spent her odd moments going to flower shops
and gift shops and other likely stores, taking orders to be shipped
next August. She'd hold her bouquet up and ask, "How much
of this will you want in season next summer?" Just about everybody said, "I'll take all you can supply!" Most never asked
the price. On her afternoons off, Mrs. Crowthers would come
back to the house with another notebook of orders.

My father, when in Philadelphia, always had some law
case on his mind, and didn't always pay attention to other things.
Now, one evening, he became aware of this sea lavender business, and he began asking questions about it. Mrs. Crowthers
went to her room and brought down her order books. My father said, "Jeehossophatts!" It was an expression we heard otherwise only at Morning River from Mr. Thomas.

Mrs. Crowthers had "invented" a company; "The Razor
Island Oceanside Garden Cooperative," and had contracted (my
father said) to supply sea lavender in bloom at so much a bunch
by mail, payment within ten days of receipt. My father also said,

"Migod!"

Then he sat for a few minutes, touching his fingers together in thought. He said, "I'll have the office register the business, if that needs doing in Maine, but I don't know what else you've got us into! We'll need a post office account number, I suppose at Monhegan or somewhere, and we'll need a bank, and as we'll need an attorney, I suppose I'll have to take the Maine bar exam again. What do you plan to ship these things in? Who makes boxes? What about labels? We'll need letterheads to dun the deadbeats! How did I get mixed up in this?"

My father was wrong about one thing: There were no deadbeats. Every store and shop we sent flowers to paid right away, and only a few of them ever took the two percent for cash.

My father had the printing done in Philadelphia, and he located a florist supply house out west that had boxes.

Han and I began our business venture with enthusiasm. We picked sea lavender every morning until every last stem had thrown its blossoms and we had the Croze Nest and the sawmill full. The sea lavender dries, so doesn't want water. We made bunches all the same size, wrapped them in tissue paper and tied a ribbon. The boxes had our "company" name—Razor Island Oceanside Garden Cooperative—and we pasted on address labels my father's office girl had typed from the list made out by Mrs. Crowthers. In just about a day and a half Han and I had quite enough sea lavender. But we hadn't used all the boxes, and my father said we couldn't quit the business until he got his money back for the boxes. Our company did make a decent penny on the venture, and we finally paid my father back what he had advanced, and had a nice bank balance. In the third August, we squared accounts and Han and I went trout fishing and had a cook out up the river.

There was one comical outcome that my father said was worth all the work. Mr. Thomas had gone over to Monhegan Island on an errand, and he came back with a registered letter. He said the postmaster had the thing for a couple of weeks and didn't know what to do with it. It was addressed to the Razor

Island Oceanside Garden Cooperative and it came from the office of the Attorney General of the State of Maine, Statehouse, Augusta. At that, my father immediately became professional, looked at the address, and gave the envelope to Han to open and to refer to the legal department. My father never laughed harder and longer than he did at that letter.

He said to begin with, it was "weasel worded." It almost, but not quite, accused Han and me of operating a greenhouse and floral supply business without a state license, of not registering our principal address and place of business, of engaging in export sales without making required reports, and failure to comply with laws about state inspections. Also, we had no state certificate to be had from the Department of Agriculture, for which application blank was enclosed and would we forward required fee of one dollar. My mother handed a glass of water to my father, and after a sip he controlled his hysterics. Mr. Thomas said, "I take it you consider this unimportant?"

My father said, "The man's an idiot. Right speed for an attorney general. He gets these complaints from a department, so he feels he should do something. I could answer him, but his next move might be even funnier. We'll see." Then he told Han and me there was nothing to worry about until we got his bill for legal advice.

And then he had all the money we made on sea lavender transferred to Han's savings account, plus all we paid him back for the boxes, and a little more, and told Han it was for her room and board "on the main" when it came time for her to go to high school.

After we'd gone back to Philadelphia for the winter, another registered letter came from the Attorney General. Mr. Thomas took care of it without bothering my father. He wrote to us: "Hope things are shaping up for a good winter down there. Things here look good. Cousin Snood got an early deer, and says mine is an eight point buck when the law goes off. Have got most of the fireplace wood under cover. Will have all by next week. Salted 20 ducks. Had a light frost Tue. Wrote dead, return to sender on another letter from Attorney General, registered. Mrs. T. sends best. Sherm."

That was the end of the Razor Island greenhouse business.

Chapter 36

STRAWBERRY FUN

My father was a member of the Masons in Philadelphia, but I don't remember that this played a big part in his city life. I do recall his coming home from the office early to get dressed in his tuxedo to go to a banquet meeting, and he was a handsome sight when the taxi came for him and he stepped out the front door. My mother straightened his tie and said, "Now don't spill wet plaster on your pants!" Otherwise, my mother said he went to meeting so seldom he didn't get the value of his dues. He said going to meeting was not required, and to leave it at that. Then my father bought Morning River Farm, and one day he and Mr. Thomas were planning something, and I heard my father say, "Where is your lodge around here?"

Mr. Thomas said, "Summertimes, we don't meet, but our lodge is over to T' Hahb'h." He said the members on Monhegan Island would all go to Lodge in one boat. The moon would be around the full and if the sea was calm it made a good evening. My father said it sounded good, but he wondered if he could work his way in. Mr. Thomas said, "Oh, I think likely." But since we always left for Philadelphia by September, nothing came of this. I think it was two summers later that we arrived at Morning River the first of June and Mr. Thomas asked at once if we'd like to go to Strawberry Festival. He said, "Coming up in two weeks; the lodge does this every year. We can all go in the sloop." So we all went to Tenant's Harbor in the sloop to the annual Masonic Strawberry Festival.

When Han and I began comparing notes, we told each other about our schools. She and I were in the same grade, she in her "disadvantaged" Monhegan Island one-room facility, and I in my very expensive and completely modern city complex. It didn't take long for me to find out that Han was so far ahead of me in all subjects, that I had nothing to crow about, and she not only spelt harder words and did stiffer number work, but she could dig clams, paint pot buoys, clean mackerel, and sail a boat. What bothered me most was that she was on the baseball team. "We play ball all winter," she said. My school didn't play baseball at all, but we had things to climb on at recess, and we did exercises when the teacher said one-two-three-four. Yes, Han said they did lose the baseball in a snowbank and had to hunt for it, but snow out to sea on Monhegan wasn't heavy. They painted the baseball yellow, which helped them find it in the drift. Han played shortstop, but batted a good average and liked left field better. Boys and girls played together, but at Strawberry Festival only girls made up the Rainbow Team, which played the Past Masters of the lodge in the annual five-inning game after the shortcakes. The Past Masters had to wear skirts, and catch and throw wrong-handed. Mr. Thomas said the umpire was always the District Deputy Grand Master, and one year Mr. Thomas had been the umpire. He said Han boo-ed him on a close call at second.

Mr. Thomas said the school sometimes didn't have nine girls for a team, so some of the Rainbow Girls would be grandmothers with arthritis. One year with low enrollment, one of the Rainbow Girls had to be a boy. Mr. Thomas also said that he didn't remember that the Past Masters ever won a game, and the score would be something like twenty-nine to two. "There's a good deal of rhubarb," he said.

We got Mrs. Crowthers into the sloop all right, and the

sail to Tenant's Harbor was easy. We had a fresh westerly, Han told me. When we got near, we found just about every boat that would float was ahead of us, and some boys with an outboard on a skiff were a taxi to bring folks ashore. There was no mooring for us, so Han and I got the anchor ready and Mr. Thomas used that. Just as we got our anchor set, Cousins Manfred and Snood arrived in Snood's power boat, and they tied to Mr. Thomas's sloop.

My father was amused at all the talk about pies. Somebody would shout, "Hi, Nell! You got my mince?" Then my father found out that the ladies don't bring pies to a strawberry festival. No matter what kind of pie you "spoke for," you got a dish of strawberries.

The festival started at the appointed time when a circle of men, all with little aprons, stood on the lodge hall lawn. One of them made a prayer, and then a man in a tall silk hat invited us all to have a good time. The Eastern Star ladies served the strawberry shortcake and poured the coffee, and I looked across and saw my father, Mr. Thomas, Cousins Snood and Manfred, and Mrs. Crowthers all wearing little aprons and eating shortcake. My mother and Mrs. Thomas were not in uniform, but they had shortcakes. Han and I sat on the lodgehall steps, along with some of her Rainbow baseball team. Han told me she never joined Rainbow; too much trouble and time to get to the mainland meetings.

There had been some youngsters romping around and making a nuisance. One of them was a squealer, and his piercing yelps were annoying. Everybody was glad when his father grabbed him by an arm, tipped him over a knee, and belted him about his manners. The kid was too surprised to bawl but he did quiet down. Then word went around that the admonisher was not the boy's father. He was just a man in the crowd that hated unchallenged squealers. Then the man handed the corrected squealer a plate of shortcake and a spoon.

People from all up and down the coast had come to the strawberry festival, some by road but more by water. They seemed to know one another, proving you can be neighbors if you live far apart. Han knew most of them. Mr. Thomas kept bringing folks to meet my father and mother, and a few people said they'd been at our dory lanch. My father was, "The gentleman from Philadelphia who has Morning River." *That* just wouldn't go away. Han noticed it, and a couple of times squeezed my hand and said, "Newcomers!" Newcomers from Philadelphia, with money.

The Rainbow Girls won again. To get nine officers, the Masons had to use their organist. Han said when the lodge didn't meet he played the piano in a Rockland movie theatre. He wore an antique hoopskirt from a very old trunk. He played third base. The man with the tall silk hat was umpire, and he favored the Rainbow Girls every time he could. The Masons had to keep their fielders' gloves on the wrong hands, and were limited about how high they could lift their skirts if they had to run. It took not quite two hours to play five innings, and the final score was announced as 28-zip. But nobody kept any score, and when Han hit her home run it took about fifteen minutes for the man with the hoopskirt to carry the ball back to the pitcher. On the way he sold a few more 25-cent chances on the Hudson's Bay striped blanket to raise money for new steps.

After the baseball game ended, there were more strawberries for the eating, and for ten cents a basket of berries could be had for preserving or eating at home. My father asked Mrs. Crowthers if she felt like jam, and when she nodded he bought three dollars' worth.

Then the man in the silk hat said Worshipful Brother Mosely expected to have fresh strawberries at his farm for at least another week, thank you all for coming, and see you next year!

People visited, and the boys with the skiff and motor taxied until the crowd thinned, and then we went out to the sloop, strawberries and all. There was a moon, and the ocean was ruffled only by a June twilight breeze. Everybody was weary from the day, and full of shortcake. Mrs. Crowthers said, "I'm glad nobody wants supper." Nobody did. After we got away from the harbor, Han and I got comfortable, back-to-back, on the sternsheets, and Han held the wheel while the sloop sailed herself. Mrs. Crowthers, in a folding deck chair, fell asleep and snored courageously. My father and mother, and Han's father and mother, spoke not a word all the way home until in Razor Island Gut Mr. Thomas said, "All right, Han—I'll take her to the wharf."

It was a wonderful day and a glorious evening, and I'll never forget Han's words when we said goodnight. Han said, "I was lucky with that pitch. I pulled the ball some."

Winnifred, on my father's office staff, was the one he trusted most to do things right, and he told her to get a dozen baseballs for the Monhegan Island school. He knew about Han's playing "scrub" in the snow all winter, but it didn't register with him until he saw Han play baseball at the strawberry festival. Now he realized the importance of baseball in the Monhegan Island educational system. He said to Winnifred, "See if you can find a sporting goods store that will mail a dozen baseballs to the Monhegan school, and I want them painted a dandelion yellow."

Winnifred said, "Certainly." That noon, lunching at the club, my father asked his friends, "I've got her in my office, but where else in this world can you find somebody that says 'certainly' to yellow baseballs?" He said many times that Winnifred was one in ten million. Later on, Winnifred did say that she wondered, but figured if my father wanted her to know, he'd have told why he wanted yellow paint. She said one store she called refused absolutely to paint the baseballs yellow, on the grounds that the Spaulding rule book forbade any color except the natural leather. Another store asked Winnifred why, and she said when she found out she'd call back. My father said "his" Winnifred was the total answer to that Hubbard man and his message to Garcia. The next summer, when my father and Cousin Snood met, Cousin Snood said, "Next time, send them balls to me. One of my pot-buoy colors is Sunshine yeller, and when the school gets a new ball, I get to paint it."

Han didn't write to me too often, but the dozen baseballs were worth a letter:

> Teacher asks me to write for everybody. Merry Christmas and thanks for the baseballs. We hung them on the tree for the school party. No snow yet, but we're ready. Cousin Snood made us a new fungo bat. It's willow and stuffed with seine cork. Keen. Everybody set for trap day. Happy New Year. Thanks again.

Chapter 37

SAM
THE HAM

One summer in particular came to a glorious finish, and we had ten more days than usual in Maine. It was the same summer that Cousin Snood told all the complaints on Monhegan Island that he and Mrs. Crowthers were planning to spend the winter together on his boat at Man o' War Key in the Bahamas. He put up a notice in the Post Office: "Wanted to rent through May—One alcohol-fuel galley cookstove with gimbals, also one commode." Anyway, that was the summer Mr. Thomas said at a flip hour, "You make a big mistake going home the end of August. If October isn't our best month, then September is. You miss the fall flowers and the color, and all the handsome days with a high sky and the birds making up to head south. Why don't you stay over a week or ten days and we'll go over into Penobscot Bay and see if the summercaters are gone?" For the next couple or three days he kept harping on this idea, and he put up quite an argument for Penobscot Bay.

"Why," he said, "you get down there around Matinicus and Criehaven, and you look out to sea, and you wonder where God expected to find left-over water for His piddlin' Pacific Ocean! That's when you realize what big means. There's all manner of places to stay, and after Labor Day we'll have everything to ourselves." Winnifred took care of everything, including my excuse for missing school. There was considerable red tape to that in the Philadelphia system, whereas Han was excused from school in a less complicated way. Cousin Snood chanced by, and Mrs. Thomas told him to tell the teacher Han would be a few days late. So a couple of days before we would otherwise have started for Philadelphia, off we went instead with the Thomases in their sloop, Han at the wheel and Mrs. Crowthers clutching the arms on her folding deck chair for dear life. We were gone nine days, including Labor Day on our first Monday. We had the ocean all to ourselves, but Mr. Thomas explained that two weeks earlier we'd be sharing it with, excuse me, ritch bitches from all over. We didn't plan to sleep on the sloop, so found a mooring each evening and went ashore to a place run by somebody the Thomases knew. Summer guests had all left, so we'd make up our own beds. Then we'd make supper on the sloop, or we'd eat with the family that ran the inn. The weather was, as Mr. Thomas promised, very different. August, with a tendency for fog and muggy days, was gone, and September was bright and clear, with fresh winds, cool but comfortable. All these people that found us bedrooms fell in love with Mrs. Crowthers, who would release her handholds on the sloop and parade into a kitchen to take over. Women who had been cooking all summer for paying guests "from away" would sit in a rocking chair and tell her in which cupboard to find the cinnamon, and which frypan to heat. On that trip, Mrs. Crowthers forgot absolutely that when she got home to Morning River, she was going to brain Cousin Snood with a clam hoe.

We had a most pleasant visit with a lobsterman friend of Mr. Thomas at Matinicus. As we arrived at the island, Mr. Thomas said, "Oh! Good! I was hoping Sam would be here!" He put the sloop alongside a lobster boat that was on mooring, and Han and I reached to hold the coaming. Mr. Thomas called, "Sam! Ahoy! Have a honk?"

This lobster boat was somewhat special. She was more like summer mahogany than a work boat, with considerable bright metal. Aloft, she had wires strung, and from under her tight sprayhood we could hear the dits and dahs of Morse Code, which I had heard once before in school when a man talked on wireless telegraphy. Sam appeared from under the sprayhood, barefooted, and recognizing Mr. Thomas said, "So, you've come to pay me all that money you owe! Never suspected it would happen. Did you mention a honk?"

After introductions, Sam said he'd hatched a pea soup with johnnycake, and every time he made a pea soup he'd be damned but a crowd appeared to help him eat it. "Han!" he said. "You've growed! Why'n't you go below and roust out some canvas stools? Didn't I hear somebody say honk?"

There may be other ways to commence, but for now this will do.

When it came time for Sam to go to high school, he picked Greely Institute, and he boarded with a family where the father was telegrapher at the railroad station. At home, in his off hours, he played with wireless, and was a ham radio operator. He taught Sam to read code, helped him make his own "rig," then Sam went to sea as a "sparks." Now retired and home again at Matinicus, Sam owned the only boat in Penobscot Bay with radio, a good many years before it was to become common on boats. It was said that he had forgotten more about wireless than Marconi ever knew. The word was that he operated on ten meters and Old Smuggler whisky, and being before his time and remote he didn't bother to take out a license. Every time he went to Rockland Harbor the Coast Guard boys would ask him to tune their transmitter, and asked him about his call letters. He would tell them he was documented, and this seemed to satisfy them. Sam did tell my father that he did have call letters, but he rarely got any calls. "I mostly listen to cheat the time," he said. He told my father, "I'm an SWL on CWO," and my father nodded as if he knew very well what that meant. Sam told us a tanker went aground one time and just for fun he went on the air and found the Boston Globe. He dotted and dashed the news, and the Globe sent him a check for fifty dollars. Sam said, "That was pretty good for five hundred words, but it's a long time out here between stories." Sam said he qualified as a member of the amateur radio relay league, but had never had a message. "I wouldn't know what to do with it!" All the time we were on his boat, his wireless kept ditting and dahing, and evidently Sam was able to read the thing and keep up a conversation at the same time. He told us it wouldn't be long before every boat we saw would have radio and the Morse code would give way to voice.

His pea soup was superb and his corn bread caused Mrs. Crowthers to ask for his recipe. Sam said, "One cup corn meal, one cup flour, one cup sweet milk, one cup sour—you must be from away!"

Mr. Thomas took us around Mount Desert Island, and we spent a night at McKinley. We saw all the big-wig summer mansions, and my father said, "There isn't one of those would tempt me to swap Morning River." Mr. Thomas said, "They're all too far away."

Mrs. Crowthers added, "I wouldn't give one house room." She also said, "It's the yellow split peas. I been using the other kind."

Chapter 38

TAMING
DEER

In the course of their getting acquainted after my father bought Morning River Farm, Mr. Thomas had said, "And you can get your deer every fall right off the porch steps." My father was of no mind to be a hunter, and wasn't interested in shooting a deer, even if the deer was "his." We learned shortly that in the down-Maine custom, all deer are possessive. Every man has his own, depending on who shot it. It turned out most of our Morning River deer really belonged to Cousin Snood, who would run in from Monhegan on the morning the season opened and get "his" deer, and often enough one of my father's deer, too. The considerable bunny swamp from which Morning River began was ideal for wintering deer, and Cousin Snood would keep tabs and count noses. Sometimes, we heard, Cousin Snood didn't wait for the law to "go off." One year a doe that had wintered in our swamp had twin fawns, and Mr. Thomas told us he had seen them not long after they'd been "dropped." From his directions, Han and I walked up along the edge of the swamp and had found them. This would be early in July and the little ones were still red and spotted, and very much in Mother's care. Han and I kept very still for a long time, until the doe made a little noise and hustled them out of our sight. Doing as Mr. Thomas told us, we found a game trail so we'd know where to look another time.

Han and I decided it can't be a great deal of fun to be a deer. The mother, every time we saw her, was perpetually in fear. She'd take a step, look in every direction, and take another step. Mr. Thomas told us she likely had nothing in the swamp to be afraid of, unless a bobcat or a wild or stray dog appeared. He said fishers had been known to kill a deer, and could easily kill a fawn, but settlers had purposely exterminated fishers a hundred years ago when they learned to attack farm animals. The same with the wolves. Han and I wondered if maybe this doe wasn't afraid of Cousin Snood. Her fawns were equally skittish, and betrayed at every moment that they were ready to vanish if their mother gave them a warning wheeze. Several times either Han or I would move, the mother would sense us, and the fawns would be gone. They'd just melt into the growth.

But methodically, doing as Mr. Thomas told us, we tamed the fawns and also the mother. We did it with saltine crackers. After we found an open space near the game trail, we left a couple of saltines on a piece of birch bark we flattened on the ground with small rocks. The next day our saltines were gone, but some droppings indicated a squirrel, and we just left two more saltines. The next day our saltines were gone again, but the bark had been disturbed and hoofprints showed a momma deer and two fawns. We replaced saltines for two more mornings.

Mrs. Crowthers reasonably asked what we were doing with the saltines, and did we want her to put us up some lunches. We told her about the fawns, and Han said before the end of the week we'd have them down in the dooryard so she could feed them. Mrs. Crowthers seemed to think deer might be something that she'd as soon not have around the dooryard.

Probably Han and I could have brought the fawns down out of the swamp sooner than the week, but Han didn't want things to go too fast. So we moved the birch bark a short distance each day, and left the two saltines that much nearer the houses. And we began leaving two saltines for each fawn, and two for Momma. By the end of the week, we did have the deer in the dooryard, and Mrs. Crowthers looked out to see Momma and her babies standing by the birch bark waiting for their crackers.

By that time, Han and I could walk almost to the animals before Momma would gurgle and end the scene. But in a couple of days Han was able to pass a saltine to a fawn, and after that the things were a nuisance, and Mrs. Crowthers, along in July, had to swoosh them out of her kitchen with a broom. She objected to the droppings they left on the floor. By that time the fawns were nearly the size of their mother, and Mr. Thomas had told Cousin Snood to find "his" deer someplace else and not go shooting the youngsters' playmates.

Chapter 39

THE
SKIN KETCH

It was our telescope, but probably an expert on such would say it was merely a very good spy-glass. When my father bought the Morning River property, the telescope was mounted on a sturdy tripod in the big window at the head of the main stairway in the big house, and the legend was that Madam Elzada would sit in a comfortable chair there and look to see if her Captain Alonzo Plaice were heading into the gut with his schooner. Mr. Thomas said this made a good yarn, and was just another of the Maine stories about widows who kept a light burning in the window. When Han and I arranged our Croze Nest and used it as our hang-out, my father said we could have the telescope and Mr. Thomas dismounted it and set it up for us. We could swivel it from almost east to almost west, and it brought in everything in that range. We could count the hairs in a fisherman's mustache sixteen miles away. We could also keep tabs on all the traffic through Razor Island Gut, and watch the daytime steamers that passed by Monhegan.

And in the routine that Han and I followed, every afternoon that was fit, we'd come up dripping wet from our swim in the millrace pool, and I'd dry Han off with one of the two towels we kept in our Croze Nest just for this. Then she'd dry me, and when that towel got a mite raunchy, she'd soap it and hang it in the millrace to wash. And as Han stood there, back to me and hunched up so I could give her a good rubbing, she'd look into the eyepiece of the telescope and give me the low-down on anything she saw. If nothing unusual appeared, Han would invent something, and she always purred like a pussycat when the towel made the small of her back happy.

Then I got to look at the ocean while she dried me, and all the wonderful things Han was able to see were gone by that time. Except for one memorable and outstanding sight which she did not make up.

It had been a beautiful day and we had looked forward in the heat to our swim. The plan was for both families to eat supper together at the big house, and Han and I would shorten our swim time and go up to set the table and help with the getting ready—and have our small flips allowed on these double occasions. Han was getting the towel and had her eye to the telescope, and she said, "Oh, Boy! Look at this ketch!"

I looked out the window and without the telescope I could see a sailboat moving west to east in our gut, and by that time in my Maine summers I knew a ketch when I saw one. Han stepped back and I looked through the glass.

She was a beautiful ketch, mahogany smooth and everything bright, and with just one jib set she was getting enough air to move in stately dignity past our estuary.

With one hand on the tiller, a grown man was standing aft without a stitch of clothes on, his feet braced apart and his head tipped up to keep an eye on the edge of his jib.

In the cockpit on a deck chair, was an equally mature woman, equally naked, her feet up on the portside rail in a frank and open manner, but she was not looking at the book in her hand as her attention had been diverted to the four naked children just forward. Three girls and a boy, and the boy had just brought in a mackerel he had caught. Han and I couldn't hear, but we could see that the woman with the book was pleased with the boy's success, and the obvious gentleman at the tiller clapped his hands in approval. Han was now back at the eyepiece, and the ketch had moved along. We swiveled, taking turns, and soon the show was over.

Han and I told about this at supper time, and perhaps some of the reaction deserves thought. Mr. Thomas said, "Sun bathing in a boat can raise a God-awful sunburn. A little late for mackerel. Are you sure it was a mackerel? Nautical nudists. Cousin Snood calls them skin boats."

My father said, "With that spy-glass you should have noticed the name of the book she was reading."

Mrs. Crowthers said, "That's terrible! I think it's just terrible when people don't keep their decency!"

Chapter 40

HAN
MATURES

There was a new urgency to get back to Morning River Farm that next spring. I'd never felt just that way before. It was because Han and I were growing up. As the day to start for Maine approached, I noticed I was irked strangely when my father said we'd take an extra day for the trip. Some years earlier there had been a lawsuit against the railroad, and he had handled it and won, and now the railroad up in Maine was being sued in a similar case. My father had promised the Maine lawyer he'd drop off pertinent papers on the way through Portland. So we stayed over and took rooms at the Falmouth Hotel, and my father met the other lawyer at the federal courthouse. My mother and Mrs. Crowthers said the Falmouth was a splendid hotel and the dining room was superb, but I wasn't happy about waiting another day to see Han. I hoped Mr. Thomas wouldn't get confused and come to Wiscasset for us on the wrong day. He didn't, and when we got to Wiscasset he was there with his sloop, and so was the man with the pick-up truck to help with our trunk and bags. I raced from the train and down the ramp to the wharf, expecting to see Han, but she wasn't on the sloop.

I went through the ritual Han insisted I use. I said to Mr. Thomas, "Good morning, Captain, request permission to come aboard, sir!"

Han had told me, "That sloop is my father's dearest thing. It's his every way and all the way. My mother won't step on it until he asks her, and I wouldn't dare. So always ask him, and wait to be bid. And that's true of any other boat," Han always said bo't, the Maine way. The way I do, now. So Mr. Thomas said, "Welcome aboard, and welcome home! Han didn't come. She'll be at the wharf."

Then the others came, and the man with the pick-up, and Mrs. Crowthers needed the usual help to get onto the sloop. This set up some squealing and giggling, and my mother said, "I guess you're never going to make a sailor."

Mr. Thomas said, "Oh, I don't know, now. I think you do some better every year! Back in seafaring days, getting aboard ship was called a tumblehome. You sort of aimed yourself, and then went over the rail in a heap. I think you did just fine, good lady!" When things were trimmed, we moved from Wiscasset down river, and Mrs. Crowthers took her usual "trick" at the wheel—a diversion Mr. Thomas felt would take her mind off the likelihood of being seasick, which she never was. There is no prettier water than that of Sheepscott Bay, and thanks to the seamanship of Mr. Thomas and Mrs. Crowthers we were soon looking at Big Razor Island and coming home.

Han was on the Morning River wharf when we turned into the estuary. There was the single finger wave that I guess only Mainers know how to make so it does the work of a welcoming anthem by a full band. My finger answered her. I turned to Mr. Thomas to ask, "May I handle the line for you, sir?" It is his sloop.

Han took my line and made it to the spile, and I went to make a blowline at the stern. Mrs. Thomas was coming along the path from the Marcoux house. The air was full of greetings. We were home!

And by now, Han was all over me. Her arms were

165

around my neck and shoulders, and her mouth was on mine with purpose. We had never done that before.

Han unwound some and said, "You took so long!" I said about as stupid a thing as anybody could manage. I said, "We spent the night in Portland."

Han said, "Did you, now?"

Everything was ready for us and it took little time to get settled in. The trunk and the bigger bags were emptied at the wharf and the contents taken to the big house by armsful. Then the trunk and bags were stored in the mill until fall. Summer began at Morning River Farm!

Han and I tidied the sloop and secured her for the night. Mr. Thomas inspected everything and said that would do for now. We'd had some snacks on the sail from Wiscasset, so it was decided to skip eating until supper, when Mrs. Thomas was serving clam cakes. Han had dug the clams yesterday. Mr. Thomas said, "Then what's holding up the flip hour?"

So in no great time at all, Han and I were in our Croze Nest, I think a bit awkward from our display of affection when we met, and for a while we just sat there holding hands, and when we tried to say anything it trailed off and we lost it. I told her I never felt this way about her before. Han said, "Me, too."

So we sat, and after a time Han said, "I've got something I want to show you."

Han said that to me many times. She knew so many things I didn't know that she always had something to show me. It might be a bobolink nest in the meadow. How to tie a knot. This time, she said, "This is special!"

I looked at her and waited, and she said, "This is extra very special!"

And she stood up and took off her shirt.

I'd seen Han with no shirt many times. Now she said, "Look at me! I'm going to be a woman!"

I saw the bulges. The nipples, like mine last fall, were not like mine now. There was more to do yet, but I could see where it was about to be done. "Isn't it all wonderful?" Han asked. She stood in front of me and lifted my hands. I said it was wonderful. Han said, "That feels nice."

Han told me, "I showed my mother the other day, and all she said was I'd have to have a bathing suit."

I said I wouldn't like that.

Han said, "I didn't plan to."

Then she said, "I'm getting hairs. Are you?"

"No."

"You will. Boys do later. It says in the book."

"What book?"

"A book up in the big house. An Elzada book. It's a doctor book." So there you have it, and after a few minutes Han put her shirt on, but she didn't button it right away.

We talked about growing up and other things, and what she'd found in the Elzada doctor's book. Han said, "Then, too, my mother tells me things." So it was Han who told me her mother had been just about Han's age now when Han was born. Han said, "My mother and my father didn't expect me. They got married on God's Tugboat before anybody knew I was around."

Then this conversation about the facts of life and the wonders of growing up was interrupted while I found out what God's Tugboat might be. Han told me the Maine Seacoast Missionary Society down east (in Bar Harbor, she thought) maintains a boat called the *Sunbeam* which cruises up and down the Maine coast and looks after folks on the islands and remote places on the main, bringing them the Gospel and other comforts, and doing all sorts of kindnesses. The seagoing minister has his navigation papers for wind and steam in all waters. The *Sunbeam* is God's Tugboat.

(Editor's Note: There have been several *Sunbeams*. *Sunbeam V*, sixty-five feet on the waterline, diesel powered and capable of a sustained eleven knots, was launched in April of 1995. Contributions to support the *Sunbeam* may be sent to the Maine Seacoast Missionary Society, Bar Harbor, Maine 04609.)

Chapter 41

THE
HEN SUMMER

Our Morning River experience with chickens lasted through one summer, or from the time my father knew we had a henhouse to the day Mrs. Thomas put our flock into Mason jars for winter purposes on Monhegan Island. The henhouse was behind the Marcoux home, and hadn't been used lately so bushes had grown up around it. It was in good shape, however, and my father had stepped in one day for a look. He saw the roosts and the row of nests and later he asked Mr. Thomas what he thought that building had been for. Mr. Thomas said, "I think it was for something that sits on a roost and lays eggs." Everything connected with our Morning River poultry business was at just about that same destructive speed.

There had been a yard surrounded by a hen-wire fence, but in disuse the wire had rusted. Mr. Thomas fixed that, and then found some laying hens from a farmer in the town of Warren. They came in a crate on the mail boat, and Cousin Snood brought them from Monhegan all cocked and primed with the information every hen farmer needs to know to succeed. They cost one dollar each for ten hens and five dollars for a rooster that was twice his own size and knew it. His hens were well aware their sole duty was to amuse him and that his gratitude

168

would be offered profusely. Meantime, he would tell them what a fine fellow he was. The first time he flew at Han, his spurs to the fore, she caught him under his chin with her toe and for twenty minutes we thought she had killed him. He didn't fly at Han again, but I was afraid of him and always made her go in the pen first. His hens were lovable ladies.

Han and I immediately became the managers of our poultry enterprises, and all we knew came from Cousin Snood, who always knew a great many things that aren't so. The rooster would run and hide when he saw Han coming, so within a couple of days she had the hens coming to meet her, and they would peck the eyelets on her sneakers until she picked a hen up one at a time and told them they were slobs. They were, as Cousin Snood thought, at the end of a clutch, so it was a good week before we saw an egg, and two weeks before they were giving us six to ten eggs a day. Cousin Snood had brought Mrs. Crowthers a porcelain hen with a lift-up cover to keep eggs in, and Mrs. Thomas had a bowl in the Marcoux kitchen for the same. A new flip sweetener was provided forthwith, we got custards, and Mrs. Thomas had to show Mrs. Crowthers how she built a custard pie up to three full inches without having it fall over.

Then the disasters peculiar (Cousin Snood said) to poultry management struck. One morning we found one of our beautiful hens dead as any beached-out mackerel in the pen, inside the wire, and she had been done in by an animal. She'd been chewed. Mr. Thomas came at Han's alarm, and said it might be a hawk, but he thought it was an owl. Didn't we close the little door last evening?

No, we didn't. Nobody told us we should close the little trap door at night. Mr. Thomas said the hens would go inside to roost, but if we didn't shut the door a raccoon could go in, too. But he didn't think this was a raccoon; the way the hen was chewed he suspected an owl. Had we seen an owl? Or a hawk?

No. And no signs of a fox or a raccoon.

Mr. Thomas went up and looked around in the sawmill, and found a steel trap with a chain. He showed Han and me how to set it on a fence post. No bait. An owl will fly in and perch to look things over, and you may find him in the morning with one of his horny talons hung up in a fatal embrace. Mr. Thomas had called that shot, but now we had nine hens. The next thing was a red squirrel.

Han saw a red flash by the feeder when she opened the henhouse door, and since we'd been closing the hatch at night I asked, "How do you suppose he gets in?"

Han said, "I guess he don't; I think he IS in." Why not? A feeder full of mash, clean water every morning, and everything cozy. Stick around and enjoy life. Han and I looked around, but found no squirrel. But the next morning we did. The squirrel, red as Han said, was by the hen-feeder hopper, very much lifeless, and his blood on the feeder, and on the litter. Then Han said, "Hey! Look here!" And there was our million-dollar rooster, huddled in self-pity in the corner, one eye puffed closed, and his handsome rose comb swelled shapeless into a bruised glob of minced meat and clotted blood. He was a mess, and he knew it. He seemed to sigh, and tried to pull himself together.

The story Han and I told, wholly conjecture, seemed plausible then and still does. Our rooster, having experienced an owl that stood taller than he did, had now a second encounter. All in the dark he had tackled the red squirrel, which had grabbed him by his beautiful topknot with one end and had scratched an eye out with the other. But the squirrel had lost. Han had the rooster in her arms, and he was contrite and subdued. I took him to the house and Mr. Thomas held him while Mrs. Thomas cleansed his hideous wounds and made him well.

So now we had a one-eyed rooster with very sore comb and wattles swollen three times, and Cousin Snood said we still had a raccoon to go.

All unbeknownst to any of us, our raccoon was already in residence. Mrs. Crowthers had tossed a handful of crumbs off our back porch, thinking the birds would soon have them, and in a few minutes she looked from the window and saw dear little Sammy Coon out there gleaning. She didn't happen to say anything to anybody about this, and she would now and then leave a goodie on the porch and then watch to see how long before the raccoon came for it. Mrs. Crowthers, being from away, didn't have a native hatred for raccoons, the dirtiest and most vicious beast in the Maine woods (as Cousin Snood was soon to tell me) and considered her friend a darling little bandit with his black mask. The cute little thing even picked up his food with his darling little hands! And the time came when the sweet little thing ripped the fence wire loose, broke the trapdoor from its little slide, and went into our henhouse to drag out a biddy all squawking and beating her wings, and the raccoon eating her as he came. The flock, including the wounded rooster, was raising ructions in the henhouse, and Mr. Thomas came on the run, a step ahead of Han.

I heard the commotion from my bed, and by the time I got downstairs the raccoon had dragged the poor biddy up to our porch, presumably so Mrs. Crowthers could watch the cute little thing eat a live hen, and just as I stepped out Han hit the raccoon with a clam hoe, and then hit the hen to end her suffering. Mr. Thomas greeted us, and Mrs. Crowthers, with, "It's all over! Han won!" But we now had eight hens and a defective rooster.

Our hen business does sound like a gruesome affair, and it was, but it wasn't all bad. The poor rooster recovered, but he never did learn to crow, and he always had a split wattle about which he talked a great deal. But Han and I did have some good moments. Up along the river, in bygone days, there was a field planted to clover. It was white clover, which makes sense. Mr. Thomas said that Jules Marcoux kept honeybees, and that honeybees are not able to work the red clover, which most farmers plant for the cattle. The bees' little snouts aren't long enough to reach into the blossoms and get the nectar. So Morning River used the white clover, which bees can handle. That field kept reseeding, and while the white clover had "run out" as Mr. Thomas put it, there was still considerable, and Han and I would walk up and cut or pull a couple of clamhods full for our hens. They ate every shred of it, and fought over it. After we did this a few times they'd be waiting for us, lined up along the wire fence, and they'd go right at it and clean it up in minutes.

When we first put our hens in the house and they began using the outdoors pen, the ground was sod and bushes had started. The hens soon took care of that. We were down to bare ground and it was scratched up. The bushes soon died. As the ground dried out, the hens began "dusting." They'd grovel and saturate their feathers with dust, and then jump and shake. Mr. Thomas said it cleaned them, and also killed lice if they had any. After that Han and I looked for lice, but didn't find any.

That was about it with our chicken business. The only time I heard Mr. Thomas speak up as if he intended to be heard and paid attention to was there on our back steps after Han swung the clam hoe. Mrs. Crowthers, attracted by the hullaba-loo, had come rushing to the porch to find out what was going on, and she saw her pet raccoon in the past tense, and Han stand-ing over him with the clam hoe ready to sock again. "Oh, my!" said Mrs. Crowthers. "The poor little thing!"

Mr. Thomas looked at Mrs. Crowthers, and perceiving her agitation, he spoke deliberately. He said, "My dear, good, lady! I beg you to ask this one-legged hen here just what she thinks of your poor little thing!" He took the clam hoe from Han, used it to gather up the raccoon, took the hen by her only leg, and walked out of sight around the building.

Before we left for Philadelphia that September, Mr. Tho-mas fixed the rest of our hens and the crowless rooster, and Mrs. Thomas and Han cooked them off and put the meat in glass jars.

And we had enough eggs for breakfasts until we left. Fact is, Mrs. Crowthers hard-boiled the last of them and we ate them on the train going home. We didn't try hens again.

Chapter 42

THE
COAST GUARD

It's enough to tell what happened, without taking sides or trying to point a moral, and if I learned something from Han's tilt with the Coast Guard that afternoon, I'll keep it to myself, and cherish it. We'd had our jump in the millrace pool to cool down, and were sitting in our Croze Nest drying off when we heard the sound of a boat engine going into neutral for our wharf. We hadn't heard any boat turn into the estuary. I buckled my pants and Han got a shirt on, and from the telescope window we saw it was the Coast Guard patrol boat. Those patrol boats are made to catch anything they chase, and under low speed don't be heard too much. Maybe Han and I were dozing from the heat, and this one sneaked in on us. We went down the ramp to the wharf.

I always wondered why all the Coast Guard boys came from Oklahoma and Wyoming, but Han said the boys near the ocean were too smart to get taken in. This time, the "boy" who talked with us was still young enough to be a boy anywhere, not much older than I, and I was probably twelve then. He looked as if he'd just shaved and didn't need to. Pink-and-white. When he saw us coming he called, "Ahoy!"

By the time Han and I got to the wharf, the Coast Guard

boat was tied to the cleat and the fellow chants, "United States Coast Guard out of Rockland, may we tie up here?"

This was really a situation. I was the innocent city boy, now and forever "from away," and Han was the complete and absolute opposite. I realized that facing this fellow she straightened up and went on a kind of defensive shift. I was brought up to respect all policemen, even the man who takes tickets at the movies, and suddenly I realized that Han didn't give a good hoot who this fellow was. I thought I felt her recoil, but she smiled and said, "Welcome aboard and at your service. Can we help you?" She stood straight.

Silent, she said it all. How might two civilian midgets with wet hair help the Coast Guard? Was the Coast Guard lost? Should we point out Rockland? The fellow asked, "Was there a lobster boat passed here within the past few minutes?"

Han took a thoughtful pose and seemed puzzled. When she spoke she was far from the Han I knew anything about. She said, "Don't rightly reck'lect it. I guess I warn't paying attention. Was she blue?" Then I caught on. I'd come to know about blue lobster boats, and Han told me the first one was yet to be painted. Mr. Thomas had said it probably was not just superstition, but in the past there was some valid reason, now forgotten, that would make good sense if anybody remembered what it was.

The fellow said, "No."

"Didn't think so," said Han. "If she'd been blue I might have noticed."

So then this fellow said, "We're looking for Ronnie Chalmers. You know his boat?"

"Eyah, she's white."

"Yes."

"What you want Ronnie for?"

"I didn't say we wanted him, Miss, I said we're looking for him."

"In here? Ron don't fish in here. If'n he was to set a trap in here them highlanders over to T Hahb'h'd skin him out and hang his scalp on the baithouse door! You know that!"

"We have reason to believe he's been this way. Now, tell me, have you seen him?"

"Nope. And he ain't been this way, not today, anyway."

"How do you know?"

"Because he went to Port Clyde this morning to get a haircut. And then he was to take his violin lesson."

When we were back in our Croze Nest and the Coast Guard boat was gone, I said, "What was all *that* about?"

Han said, "No idea! But when I see Ron he'll have an explanation. He lives two houses from us, and Ron and my father used to seine together, some."

"How'd you know he went to Port Clyde for a haircut?"

"He didn't. His wife Muriel always cuts his hair. She cuts my father's hair, too. No need to go to the main for a haircut. Who cuts your hair?"

"A barber in Philadelphia."

"How much?"

"Don't know—my father pays him."

"It's worth every cent. Sometimes Muriel just bootchers my father."

We never heard why the Coast Guard was looking for Ronald Chalmers that afternoon. My father, the lawyer, questioned the reluctance to take the Coast Guard seriously, perhaps thinking Han had been needlessly unpatriotic, but Mr. Thomas said it was Island manners and others would do the same. He said Ron was a good boy and didn't need pickin' on. Mr. Thomas said, "He prolly left a nun buoy on the wrong hand."

Chapter 43

OUR
EIGHTH VISIT

The trunk and bags had gone ahead to the railroad station and we were waiting for the taxi to come for us. This would be our eighth summer at Morning River Farm in Maine, and the excitement that went with our trip in earlier years had settled into a pleasant routine, entirely because of Winnifred. Even Mrs. Crowthers, afraid of trains and petrified of boats, was relaxed by Winnifred's efficiency. At the station to see us off, Winnifred had passed my father her last note of instruction: "Don't buy morning paper on train; Mr. Barter will have *Bangor Daily* in pick-up truck." It was so. Mr. Barter was the Wiscasset fisherman Mr. Thomas had asked to meet us at the train and take us and our luggage to the Southport Bridge, where Mr. Thomas would be waiting with his sloop. Mr. Barter was there, with the newspaper under his arm.

Winnifred was black, and that was the only reason she never came to Maine. It was her reason and she said she'd be uncomfortable among so many northerners. My father told her the only northerners she'd see at Morning River would be the Thomases and Mrs. Crowthers, but she still wouldn't go to Maine with us.

So thanks to Winnifred, who brought us back to Philadelphia in September as artfully as she took us to Maine in June, the trips both ways were uneventful, and as this eighth trip began I became aware that there was something different. This awareness began when I wrote Han a letter about a week before we left Philadelphia. I'd never done that. I told her we were getting ready and when we'd leave; something Winnifred had already conveyed to Mr. Thomas. I said I was looking forward, and at the end I wrote, "All my love." And I was well aware that I looked forward most eagerly to seeing Han, and that all my love was for her. I mailed the letter with allowance for the Monhegan mail boat, and from that moment endured a new kind of impatience that was to end only with seeing Han again on the wharf at Morning River.

Mr. Barter turned out to be the gentleman with the salt-crusted pick-up by the Wiscasset station with a Bangor newspaper under his arm, and a demon mad man when it came to teaming a Chevrolet pick-up. He deftly got our luggage, us, and Mrs. Crowthers onto, into, and about his vehicle, and then tooled through Edgecomb, the Boothbays, and Juniper Point like a lost tornado on its way to Kansas, an expression sometimes used by Mrs. Crowthers for a dither. It was a great relief to find Mr. Thomas was waiting.

And as a smart morning breeze had stirred itself to welcome us, his sloop made a quick run to sea and we burst into Razor Island Gut before Mrs. Crowthers had time to take her Benzedrine tablet. Han was on the wharf.

There were some preliminary greetings, and as Mr. Thomas tossed a fender overside and brought the sloop to a nudge, I passed a line to Han and she made it to a cleat.

Han did this all in one motion, so she turned completely around as if to mean, "Here I be!" Then with a jump she cleared the coaming and was with me on the sloop. We had our arms around each other, and it was the first time Han and I had been that close together since last September! Han kissed me, but not on my cheek.

She kissed my mother and father and Mrs. Crowthers on

their cheeks, and then gave Mr. Thomas a hug. Next came putting things ashore and then taking everything to the two houses. Mrs. Thomas came to help, and said she'd started supper for all hands. Mrs. Thomas hugged and kissed me, too. Kissed me on the forehead.

Chapter 44

CROZE
NEST TALK

All along the Maine Coast the ceremonies of opening and closing the summer places are a bother. Water pipes are drained in the fall and turned on in May. Mr. and Mrs. Thomas opened and closed for us, so when we came and went we had little to do and moved in or out quickly. The dishes that had wintered on cupboard shelves had been washed and the table set for seven. The usual two-family lobster feed to celebrate our arrival would follow the flip hour, and because it was a celebration session Han and I would be permitted flips. To the others, this might be much as before, but to me and to Han there was a difference. As I opened my suitcase to put things in drawer and closet, I took up my swimming trunks and laid them on the bed. Han and I would get acquainted again. Hadn't I written, three days before we left Philadelphia, telling Han I was coming? She knew that, because my father had already written to her father (or Winnifred had) but I had never written such a letter to Han before, and hadn't I written at the end, "All my love"? Han and I were growing up. Had grown up. "All my love!" The lovely May morning on which we left Philadelphia was now a beautiful June day in Maine. I walked across from the big house to the sawmill, spoke kindly to the chipmunk waiting for me on the platform, and opened the side door into our Croze Nest, where I knew Han would also be waiting. She was.

She was sitting on the edge of the bunk-bed, her elbows braced on the mattress-pad, and she was wearing a bathing suit. I stood by the door to look at her, and I couldn't remember if I'd ever seen Han in a bathing suit. I decided I hadn't. My greeting to Han was certainly a dandy. I said, "I got swim togs, too!" Han looked down at herself, as if wondering what I, the idiot, was talking about, and said, "Oh, yes!" Otherwise, we didn't discuss swim togs.

I walked towards her, and she said, "When we hugged on the wharf, did you get all whiffled up, too?"

"Yes, I did."

"I did. I thought I would, but I wasn't sure what I was supposed to expect. Did you like?"

"Yes."

"Me, too. Finest kind! Did you jump up and bark?"

"No, but I started to."

I won't try to remember what Han and I said, or how we said it, but we got acquainted again, and when we had our swim we left the bathing suits on the nail in the wall. I guess we did look each other over to make up for a long winter. And when Han stood by the telescope and I rubbed her with the towel I got her to giggling so she couldn't stop and she wouldn't tell me what was so funny. Then we put on our shirts and pants and sneakers, and walked hand-in-hand over to the Marcoux house where Mrs. Thomas was about to put eight two-pound lobsters into the steaming pot of sea water. That figures one apiece but two for Mrs. Crowthers, and Mrs. Crowthers was teary-eyed again thinking about putting those poor things into that boiling water. She'd get that way every time we had boiled lobsters, even though everybody told her she needn't feel sorry, the lobsters are used to it.

Chapter 45

BY WIRELESS

It was coming up to the end of what would be our last happy summer at Morning River Farm. August can be kind, or it can hover in with fog like a hen settling down on her eggs. The wild blueberries had been plentiful, and Mrs. Crowthers and Mrs. Thomas had been generous with muffins and pies. The sea lavender had performed on schedule, and Han and I were again glad we had only to pick for the immediate vases, although we did bring Mrs. Crowthers a huge bouquet she would pass to friends in Philadelphia. We also put a big wad in a can on our Croze Nest table, expecting as usual to enjoy them another summer. It was still some days too early to think of packing to go home, but Mrs. Crowthers was about to begin to start to commence. It was August, and what little fog a morning brought would scale off during breakfast, and crickets chirped as crickets do.

And on that very day, Winnifred, down in Philadelphia, broke a rule. The rule was that laid down by my father about the sacred solitude of his Maine vacation. Under no circumstances was he to be disturbed by any intrusion of his Philadelphia affairs. It was a rule not likely to be broken. Even a letter had to wait on the mail boat to Monhegan Island. There was no way, really, to intrude. But Winnifred suddenly was obliged to intrude, and the reason was a letter from the Bingham Associate in Bingham, Maine, that Mayfield Plantation had unexpectedly come on the market and my father had ten days to take up his option.

You must always allow for coincidence, which never announces the next move. Oh, yes, said Winnifred to herself as she reached for her telephone. To the voice that replied, Winnifred said, "Uncle Ben, do you remember about that radio operator up in Maine?"

Winnifred's Uncle Ben was a ham radio operator, and he did remember about Sam the Ham, who lived on a lobster boat and listened to short wave to "cheat the time." Winnifred reminded her uncle that this would be a dot-and-dash matter, and her Uncle Ben went on the air with a CQ. So Sam the Ham, at Matinicus, finally got an Amateur Radio Relay League message, and it turned out he did know what to do with it. A little after noon that same day Cousin Snood tooled his power boat to our wharf at Morning River, where Han and I were picking over blueberries, and he said, "I figured this might be important." He also said, "Why'n't I take a box o' them up so Mrs. Crowthers can make me a pie to take back?"

The message told my father the Bingham option was open, and he asked me if I'd like to go up to Bingham and Mayfield with him for a couple of days. He said Cousin Snood was coming in the morning to take us over to Wiscasset.

Chapter 46

THE OCCASION

That had already been a very busy day. Han and I started by giving the sloop a cleaning. After the lobster season ended Mr. Thomas had beached her out and given her a coat of copper, but now he wanted to paint the rest of her, and Han and I gave her the Clorox and twice-over. When we tidied the cuddy we found the two bottles of Black Diamond Mr. Thomas had forgotten about, and we called to ask if he'd like a honk. He said, "Only if Cousin Snood comes!" The suggestion was enough so Han and I kept looking down the gut expecting to see Cousin Snood coming by, but he didn't. Afternoon we picked some blueberries and then picked them over, and another thing we did was replace the lanyard that held the sloop's wheel on course. Han did it, but she took the winding apart a couple of times to make me do it, and that took some time. It was one of those sailor's jobs that mustn't slip, and Han made me keep at it until I had it right. Mr. Thomas came and checked the lanyard and said we'd done more than enough for one day. I remember Han said about the lanyard, as she said to me so many times about so many things, "It's easy when you know how!" So we'd kept busy and put our cleaning tools away, and then went up to our Croze Nest for our swim. We sat on the bunk-

bed a while and had another talk. Han told me that for two summers she had been reading the doctor books in the Elzada library, and during the winter she got others from the state library.
"I wanted to know what was going on with me," she said. "And
I can tell you what goes on with you, too. Girls grow up before
boys do. I can have babies, and I can make you do the most
wonderful things." We sat quietly for some time. And Han said,
"Will you help me?"

Now, hadn't my father told me all about this? So I knew
about Mrs. Thomas and how Han was born when her mother
was only fifteen and now I was assuring myself that Han
wouldn't do anything like that with me! Not Han. Never! And
Han and I were so close. Han said, "Wouldn't you like?"

"More than anything else."

"Me, too."

And Han said, "You can. It will be all right."

Han was to have supper at the Marcoux house and she
didn't know what her mother was making. At our house, Mrs.
Crowthers was having one of her shepherd pies. Some day I
may get out a cook book that tells all the things Mrs. Crowthers
shouldn't, couldn't and wouldn't cook, but her shepherd pie
won't be in it. That was delicious. We looked forward to one.
So Han and I waited for suppertime, and she told me there was
a medical doctor who came from Hartford in September and
October to paint and for the last couple of years she'd stop and
talk with him on her way home from school. She'd ask him
about things she'd been reading in the books. She'd also ask
her mother, and sometimes the teacher. Han told me about her
privilege days, and how she was keeping a calendar. Han promised me she'd never do the way her mother did.

In spite of the shepherd pie, I wasn't excited about supper, but so nobody would notice I had my mind on something
else I had a second helping, and then Mrs. Crowthers had a real
pie, a blueberry pie. In Philadelphia we never got pie, possibly
because Mrs. Crowthers made a pie crust like cement. Lately,
though, she took a tip from Mrs. Thomas and worked in some

chicken fat, so her pie crust was very good, and I had to have a piece of her hot blueberry before I went back to our Croze Nest. Han was there, and we spent the night.

There was nothing new about that. We'd spent many nights together but never before for this reason. Han went on to tell me things she'd read in the doctor books, and I realized she was reciting from memory. I said, "You sound like you'll be a doctor."

Han said, "I been thinking about that, but I think perhaps a nurse. We get along pretty well with the mainland doctors, but we sure do need a good nurse out on the island. I'd like that." And Han talked some more about what the books said on boys and girls and growing up until she whispered in my ear, "Now, don't be afraid."

I certainly was not afraid. Neither was Han.

In the morning, Han said, "I thought it was going to hurt, but it didn't hurt. I guess you couldn't really hurt me anyway; I was too happy. It might have hurt if I'd been thinking hurt. Did you like?"

"Yes."

Han said, "We better get breakfast. Cousin Snood will be there."

"Cousin Snood?" I hadn't remembered that Cousin Snood was coming to take my father and me to Wiscasset. We were going to Bingham to buy a slate quarry. In the Croze Nest door Han kissed me, and then we closed the Croze Nest door.

185

Chapter 47

TO
BINGHAM

Morning River Farm was my introduction to Maine, and nothing, ever, will diminish my love for Maine's Atlantic Coast and the people who live on it, but had I been introduced to Maine by her wilderness, I would be equally partial to the lakes and rivers and mountains and forests. Coming by train and boat, and both, from Philadelphia does not really inform you that Morning River Farm is such a small sample of Maine. The ride to Bingham with my father was an eye-opener, and as the miles opened before us and then were behind, I lost count of the towns we came upon, each of them, it seemed, in the deep Maine woods. I had been well informed by my father about William Bingham and his prodigious "holdings," and it was hard to believe one man could own so much that is all his and so beautiful.

My father wasn't sure if Mr. Bingham had ever troubled to run up to Maine to see what he owned, but he thought he did. From our train ride we saw only some of Bingham's Kennebec Purchase, but he also had his Penobscot Purchase, in eastern Maine, and that would have included Morning River Farm except that Jabez Knight and Jules Marcoux already owned that, with deeds from the English and the French crowns. Compared to Jabez and Jules, Senator Bingham was from away. My father thought it was nice that the people of the town of Bingham named the town for him, but asked me to remember that Senator Bingham owned many towns as well as Bingham, and that he also owned the Enchanted. Both of them. The townships of Lower Enchanted and Upper Enchanted. "Happy the man who owns The Enchanted," my father said. His associate said we could ride up to see The Enchanted if we wanted to, "It's just up the road."

But we didn't. It was a revelation to ride along in the train and for every farm and every village, to see miles of woodlands. We passed many fields of corn, and my father said it was sweetcorn, to be packed in tin cans. Then he pointed out a factory for packing sweetcorn, and said a town might have one church, but it would have ten cornshops, as Maine people call them. All would be running day and night when the corn is being harvested, in just a few days now.

We were on the first train of the day, so brought the morning newspapers and the mail to each town. A few people would get on or get off, and I was interested that the conductor knew everybody. He'd take up a ticket and then pause to talk. We changed trains two or three times, but the train we changed to was always waiting for us. We had a lunch from Mrs. Crowthers, but we also stopped at some junction to eat at a restaurant. Passengers and train crew all had the same thing, which was "the dinner," and it was a delicious meatloaf. The conductor asked the man if his meatloaf was made with deer meat, and the man said, "No, that's next week."

We rode along the Kennebec River for miles, and it is a pretty river. It was exciting, because the past winter we had studied in school about the march on Quebec during the Revolutionary War, and somehow I hadn't thought of this in terms of Maine. It was hard to picture this beautiful river and it's banks in cold weather, when the army passed, when everything was warm and lush for us.

Bingham, when we got there, didn't seem to me to be much of a place, but alongside the river was one factory that sent up a huge cloud of steam. The main street had stores, and then the forest began. My father's real estate associate was at the railroad station to meet us, and turned out to be the man who ran the sawmill that was making all the steam. It was a veneer mill and had a "hot pond" to soak the big hardwood logs before they were processed.

Just before we came to Bingham, the conductor came to tell us the next stop was ours, and he asked my father who he traveled for. My father laughed, and said he was a scout for the Athletics. So the conductor said, "You don't say! I guided Connie Mack one fall. Got him a good ten-point buck! He came to Lloyd Bagley's camp at The Forks, and Lloyd sent for me as he had a special sport. Wonderful man! I think that was 1910, maybe eleven. Never had a gun in his hand until I showed him how to load. Nice to talk!"

My father's associate took us to The Yellow Bowl where we had a good supper and a double bed, and said he'd come to have breakfast with us and drive us up Mount Hunger to see the Bingham lot.

So it was, but I had only Han on my mind, and I was so lonesome for her that two or three times my father put his hand on my shoulder and said, "You all right?" After I got in bed I thought I wasn't going to go off to sleep, but the mill whistle woke me and it was time for breakfast. I had a yellow bowl of oatmeal porridge with cream and molasses, two fried eggs, sausages, hashed brown potatoes, hot cream-tartar biscuits with some maple syrup, and a piece of rhubarb pie. My father had the same, but without pie. His associate had the same, but with two pieces of pie. None of the men we saw in Bingham was wearing a hat. They all had caps, some with the earmuffs tied up with string for the summer. My first impression of Bingham had been negative; I revised it. And then we started up Mount Hunger.

The road goes right uphill from the Bingham Main Street, and at the very peak of Mount Hunger the old slate quarry is in the woods on the left hand. The associate stopped his pick-up and set the hand brake just before the road starts down the eastern side. The view ahead was incredibly beautiful. Through scattered wispy mist-clouds the sun hadn't yet dissolved, was Kingsbury Pond, which the associate said was good togue water, part of the Bingham lands, and probably in Piscataquis County. We, he knew for a fact, were in Somerset County. He could drive partway to the old slate quarry, but we'd have to walk the rest. Road had washed out years ago.

My father had convinced himself that he would like to own a bit of the William Bingham purchases, and he was now being hard to de-convince. So we drove a short distance on the derelict quarry road, passing the dump where inferior slate had been left in piles, and then walked. The quarry itself was forbidding, and the edge lined all the way around by mature spruce trees, dark and somber and suggesting grim terror in a spooky ghost story. I didn't go near the edge, and was truly afraid of the stagnant water with its yellow-green slime. Were an animal to stumble in, he could never climb the steep slate sides to get out. I actually had bad dreams later about sliding into Mr. Bingham's quarry! I was always relieved that my father and his associate felt the title to the slate quarry in Mayfield was probably fogged in the past, and they decided not to risk any venture capital. The associate said, "We logged the lot off last time it was cut, and we had no luck finding an owner."

After leaving the quarry, we went downhill towards Kingsbury Pond, which quickly ceased to be a bit of crystal in the green of a morning lawn, and was a lake a little over a mile long. The togue, my father's associate said, is a trout and everywhere else except in Maine is called a lake trout. The eastern brook trout, which also lives in Maine lakes, is never called a lake trout because of that but to Maine people is always a brook trout, even if he weighs in at eight pounds. And the trout Han and I caught in Morning River are brook trout, brookies, or square-tails. The togue has a forked tail. And as the associate explained about these different trouts, I thought, there; now I know something about fish that Han doesn't know! Han hadn't said goodbye when we left to go to Bingham. I hadn't seen her that next morning. Was she all right? And I wanted only to get back to Morning River to Han. I looked to see what my father was writing on his pad of paper, and it was Naymaycush. That's the scientific name for the togue in Kingsbury Pond.

The associate drove us to Greenville, which is on Moosehead Lake, and by another route and different trains we started back to Morning River. Moosehead Lake is magnificent—I think a better word than beautiful—and has some good sized boats, used in lumbering, and also a great many small craft for sports fishing. Also, seagulls just like ours at Morning River and Razor Island Gut. I saw my first American Indian at Greenville, a good-looking man who reminded me of Cousin Snood except that Cousin Snood doesn't walk ding-toed. My father's associate thought Indians toe in because of so many centuries of wearing moccasins. This Indian I saw certainly toed in, and he was wearing a dark suit with a felt hat, carried a briefcase, and was eating an ice cream cone. My father said, "If it wasn't for that ice cream, I'd ask him if he practices law."

The Canadian Pacific tracks from Halifax to Vancouver go through Greenville, and my father wanted to see a train go by. The big passenger trains with sleepers pass in the night, but we did see a long freight train at Greenville Junction and my father really wasn't ready for it. I guess he thought only the Pennsy would have anything like that.

It was a long and slow ride back to Morning River, and back to Han. It was close upon dark when Mr. Thomas started from Wiscasset to Razor Island Gut, but time enough left if the wind held. It did. After we were ashore my father said, "Wonder what ailed Sherm Thomas. Did you notice? I thought he was short with us."

I hadn't noticed that, as I was wondering why Han hadn't been on the wharf to take a line.

Chapter 48

MRS. THOMAS COMFORTS

Mrs. Crowthers had supper ready and we weren't too late, but I had no appetite for want of Han. My mother noticed and asked if I were all right and I said I was. I ate enough to prove I was fine and dandy, and then changed to my Morning River duds and headed for our Croze Nest. Han, I reasoned, would be on the bunk-bed ready to take off her bathing suit and go swimming. When I opened the door to step in, all my misgivings fell apart and I was all right. In the half light of the lingering day, I saw her on the bed-bunk as I supposed, and everything—everything—was all right.

It wasn't Han.

It was her mother. I realized that only when she spoke. She said, "Han isn't here."

The all-gone feeling in the pit of my gut made me hold the door latch so I wouldn't fall. I looked to see if Han's bathing suit was on the nail, and in the dusk could see that it was. I said, "What's wrong?"

Following my glance, Mrs. Thomas saw the bathing suit and said, "Han's not here."

"Where is she?"

Mrs. Thomas patted the mattress-pad beside her and

beckoned me. I swayed when I walked over, and she took my arm to help me sit on the bed. She dropped her hand to rest it on my knee, and then she squeezed as if to prepare me for bad news. I think she tried to kiss me on the cheek or forehead, but I'm not sure. I sensed that I was being comforted. I asked again where Han was.

"She's not coming." Then she said, "Han's okay."

Mrs. Thomas had an arm around my shoulders and the other hand on my knee. She tightened the arm to encourage me, and patted my knee. I supposed she was telling me to be brave, and then I reconciled all this with the way my father said Mr. Thomas had acted when he met us at Wiscasset. What was wrong? Again, Mrs. Thomas said Han was okay.

"Where is she?"

"She's on the Island. She's married."

That was it.

Mrs. Thomas pulled me towards her and said, "You'll find somebody else! You won't see Han again."

Who would somebody else be?

Mrs. Thomas said, "I'm sorry." She patted my knee.

She said, "Han told me the next morning. It happened with Han's father and me. He's a boy on the island who asked her last winter. He's a good boy. And you know as well as I do that your father would never let you marry Han. We talked it all over, and Han said all right. The *Sunbeam* was in, and there you have it. I really am sorry!"

I had nothing to say, and perhaps Mrs. Thomas was waiting for me to say it. I don't know. She said nothing, and we just sat there, her arm over my shoulder, and I numb and weak, and I was thinking how my father said Han might be family some day and how he deeded her a little corner of Morning River Farm and set up a tax fund. And I thought how Han had told me not to be afraid and that it would be all right. Mrs. Thomas tightened her arm on my shoulder.

I said, "Han isn't going to have a baby."

Mrs. Thomas said, "Maybe. We'll see."

"Well, she isn't."

"How would you know?"

"Because Han said so."

"How would she know?"

"If Han didn't know she wouldn't have said that. She told me not to be afraid." And I came to realize that Mrs. Thomas was holding me against her, her arm firm around my shoulder. The two top buttons on her shirt were open. When I put my hand inside her shirt she patted my knee. I accepted the invitation.

We didn't talk after that. Not too long before that when Han and I were talking about growing up, Han had said that from what she heard from her room in the night, her mother was "hotter'n a skunk." Han had said she'd like to be the same way. No comment from me about that, but I can tell you that Mrs. Thomas, also, told me not to be afraid. And a moment later she said, "You're big!"

When the State Highway Commission put a sign on the Southport bridge, posting the gross weight limit, Cousin Snood said, "That's a good thing to know!"

Chapter 49

MR. THOMAS TALKS

I guess I can say I don't know who I was, but I wasn't myself, and I moped around until my mother asked, "What's the matter anyway? Are you all right?" My father had asked me that on the train ride to Bingham, and then when Mr. Thomas had been short with him he began to wonder. He said to my mother, "Yes, he's all right, but I'm beginning to think he has something he'd like to tell us." So I told them how Han and I had snuggled, but nothing about how Mrs. Thomas and I had done the same, and I said they'd got Han married to a boy on Monhegan Island and Mrs. Thomas had told me I'd never see Han again. My father said, "Do you want to?"

I said of course I did, that I didn't believe what Mrs. Thomas had told me about Han's going to have a baby, and I ought to hear what Han has to say. I said, "Han won't lie to me. She's not having a baby."

My father said, "When did you say all this happened?"

"The night before we went to Bingham."

"How do you know she's not having a baby?"

"Because she told me it would be all right."

"How would she know that?"

"She's read all the doctor books upstairs."

My father said, "Maybe I'm beginning to understand a few things."

I'd forgotten Mrs. Crowthers was still with us, and now she said, "Well, I'm certainly glad for that, because I don't!"

My father asked me a few questions, and in his lawyer's way he made it easy for me to answer. Although there was nothing really easy for me about all this. But I didn't say one word about doing anything except talk with Mrs. Thomas.

My father stood some time looking out the window, and then he said to my mother that he supposed it would be the next thing to have a talk with Mr. Thomas. But my mother said, "Not now. Things have been so happy here all these years, and a wrong word in haste could spoil that. Sleep on it. Let him sleep on it."

That's what he did, anyway. Except that he didn't sleep. Wide awake, I looked out my bedroom window at the dark and I was awake when the sun came up. Well before breakfast time I heard Mr. Thomas, down in the kitchen, call to my father, and my father answered, "One minute, Sherm!" When I got out of bed a few minutes later I saw them aboard the sloop, down at the wharf. They were sitting knee to knee on the sternsheets, talking. Mrs. Crowthers fed my mother and me. And herself.

Chapter 50

THE WAY
IT WAS

It was well into the forenoon when my father came from the sloop up to the house, but Mr. Thomas stayed on the sloop, just sitting there and looking at nothing. Mrs. Crowthers made another breakfast but none of us ate, and only my father said he wasn't hungry. He also said, "Mrs. Crowthers, if you love me, find a honk!"

Mrs. Crowthers was gone all of ten seconds and came back with a bottle of Old Crow. She said, "Cousin Snood gave this to me and said to keep it for an emergency, and I guess we've got one." My father said, "I think you'll never have a better." He honked and passed the bottle back with the cap off so Mrs. Crowthers could honk. She said, "Thanks, but I already honked in the pantry."

My father said Mr. Thomas had talked with him easily enough and wanted to talk. He said Mr. Thomas had wanted to talk to somebody for a long time. "He's a sad man," he said. "He's put on an act and kept things down inside." Mr. Thomas had recited to my father how there had been a hurry-up wedding when he was told little Han was on the way, and how happy that made him, and then how things had come apart when little Han took a few more days than advertised. But Mrs. Thomas made a good wife and mother, and was a rousing good thunder bumper when it came to her evening chores. I couldn't say so, but I agreed with that, and I heard Mrs. Crowthers say, "Gracious!"

Mr. Thomas had said his wife came to him about noon that day to tell him Han was to have a baby and they had to take her to Monhegan to find "the young man," and make arrangements. My father said Mr. Thomas was matter-of-fact about all this and didn't seem at all surprised to hear his wife's daughter had been indiscreet. My father said "indiscreet," but I wonder if Mr. Thomas did.

My father said that's about all he got from Mr. Thomas, who did take Han and her mother to Monhegan, but it was breezing up and he wanted to get the sloop back to Morning River before dark. The *Sunbeam* was at Monhegan, and the minister said he'd take care of everything, and that was the sum and substance. Mr. Thomas had told my father, "I got some things from the house and went back the next day and stayed for the wedding. He's a good boy. Known him all his life. Lobsters. Has a good house and his own boat."

I knew my father had left out some parts of the story to spare me, and also my mother and Mrs. Crowthers, but he finished with, "So, I guess you'll be father to Mr. Thomas's grandchild!" Mrs. Crowthers said, "My, my!" And my mother said, "What a dirty trick on that poor boy!"

And I was the only one who had anything important to say, and nobody wanted to listen to me. I said it, all the same: "Han isn't going to have my baby!"

My father, pondering the rules of evidence, paid no attention whatever to my blunt and rash denial, as far as the words went, but when I began to cry he pounded a fist into the other hand and came right to me. He held me, and I cried. I cried as I had as a baby, and as I hadn't in years. As I hadn't, in fact, since I knew Han! My father was saying, "Go ahead, son. Get it out. It's going to be all right!" But it would never be all right, and it couldn't be all right. Han wasn't going to have my baby.

*   *   *

I sobbed and my father held me tight and said things, and I got hysterical and couldn't stop. Mrs. Crowthers brought me a cup of tea. She said, "You need something in your guzzle-goo. Try this—it's tea!"

I managed to say I hated tea.

"You'll like this; Cousin Snood sent it." I did like it, and the Old Crow stayed hot after the tea had cooled in my guzzle-goo. Mrs. Crowthers said, "I tell you what, good people, and you can give me an A-plus. Young Miss Han didn't go to that awful island to marry any lobster fisher without something that made her do it. Something happened that nobody has told me about, or I can't guess. Whatever it was, I'll find out when Cousin Snood comes for flip. He's due."

But we didn't have to wait for Cousin Snood.

Chapter 51

ETHAN DERNLEY REBUILDS THE SLOOP

Two or three times in recent summers Mr. Thomas had told my father he wanted to put his sloop into a boatyard for a good check-up and repairs if needed. But he hadn't done it. Now, with our big shake-up over Han, and with the Thomases going back to the island, my father thought it would be a nice gesture to have the sloop looked at and maybe sweeten any sour thoughts Mr. Thomas might have. So as soon as we got back to Philadelphia he turned this over to Winnifred.

My father never brought any of his office business home, any more than he took any law practice to Maine on his vacation, but now and then some unrelated thing would make amusing supper talk, and his story of how Winnifred met Ethan Dernley was maybe his best. It's about rebuilding the sloop.

Winnifred never wasted time, never permitted diversions, and stuck with something started until it was finished. On the morning she began on the sloop she found a special telephone information operator who stuck with her until she had what she wanted. They began with marine insurance agents in the Boston area, and continued to Portsmouth, New Hampshire, Portland, Maine, and Rockland, Maine. Now Winnifred had a list of boatyards, storage facilities, and boatwrights, and before long

Winnifred was convinced she should talk to a Mr. Ethan Dernley at Broad Cove Harbor, Maine. She found that this was on Thompson Long Island, and not too far by water from Monhegan Island. And Morning River Farm. The operator now rang the Dernley number.

Winnifred had been practicing her introductory remarks. She had a feeling a man so highly regarded by the yachting trade and related services might be hard to approach and her opening words might be important to his personal secretary. The gentleman who answered her ring, however, was pleasantly disposed. He said, "Dernley bo'ts. Ethan here."

Winnifred said, "Good afternoon, Mr. Dernley, I've been given your name by a number of boating people who regard you and your work highly, and I'm calling about some repairs to a sailboat."

Mr. Dernley said, "One minute!" He was back in a few seconds, and he said, "Sorry! I had to shut off the benchsaw! Now, what was that again?" Winnifred said she was calling from Philadelphia.

"Nice place. I been there. What was that stuff they gave us to eat? Straddle, was it? I liked it, but Irene didn't care for it a little bit."

"Scrapple," said Winnifred.

"I guess so. What can I do for you?"

"I'm hoping you can do some work on a sailboat."

"Can't help you a mite. We're loaded with work. Got more than a man on the town. I've had to hire a man to come from Boothbay and whittle me a button for the baithouse. What is she?"

"The boat?"

"Eyah. She in Philadelphia?"

"Oh, no. She's at Monhegan Island."

"You don't say! Sailbo't, you say?"

"Yes. She's a lobster boat there."

"Then you got to be talking about Sherm Thomas's sloop. I know that bo't. Know Sherm. She's a MacLean sloop, built on Bree-m'n Long Island. Pretty craft. What's wrong with her?"

"We don't know that anything is. But we'd like her checked out and repaired if needed."

"You winter in Philadelphia?"

"Yes. And I summer here, too. I work for the gentleman who has the Morning River Farm."

"Oh, HIM!"

"Yes. And so does Mr. Thomas. When he isn't fishing, that is."

"Eyah. Well, I can't do a thing. My place is so full of bo'ts I can't shut the doors, and the yard's full, and they're bringing more and leaving 'em on the beach. I'm sorry, but that's the story. Is she in the water?"

"Mr. Thomas's boat?"

"Eyah. The sloop."

"Yes. But Mr. Thomas isn't fishing now."

"I know; it's off season. Do you think she's ready to sail to Broad Cove Harbor?"

Winnifred said, "I suppose so, but you said . . . ."

"You don't want to believe one word I say. I'm known as a liar as far east as Dingwall. We got a new Able Down East Express sitting here and Irene's been teasing for a ride. I'll let her take me over to Munhiggin first thing and I'll sail the sloop back. Be good to get away from the bo'tyard for a few hours. What's your number there in Philadelphia, you said it was?"

When Winnifred reported this to my father he said he shook his head and asked her if she "closed." Winnifred said she thought so. And she said, "Ethan said he'd be in touch, and I'm sure he knows. I think he must be a wonderful man, and a happy man. He said he'd call in a week with an estimate, and I told him to never mind, just do a good job and look to me for his money."

My father told Winnifred, "You closed."

Winnifred said, "Ethan isn't about to abuse me."

I might as well add now that Ethan just about rebuilt the Thomas Sloop, as he found some faults he hadn't expected, but

201

he also took time to make some changes that would help with the clam-bake side of the business. For one thing, he put in a head, so the customers no longer needed to come all the way to Morning River Farm to use the backhouse he had in the bushes on our shore. Winnifred said Ethan was most genteel when he explained to her what a head is.

Chapter 52

HAN COMES AGAIN

But before we went home to Philadelphia, I saw Han. And her mother! Mrs. Thomas had told me I'd never seen Han again, and I should have known she'd be wrong. She was wrong. I did see Han again, and this time would be the last time. I hadn't been to our Croze Nest since I'd found Mrs. Thomas there, and I'd sort of decided I wouldn't go again, ever. If I started to go, which I did many times, I'd walk up along the river instead, and cut back towards the house and skip the Croze Nest. And then, one afternoon, I didn't walk up the river. I have no idea why I didn't. But I didn't, and I went in and Han was there.

She was sitting on the bunk-bed as naked as I ever saw her, but she had her bathing suit across her knees.

She didn't speak; nor did I.

I walked to her, picked up the bathing suit, and tossed it aside. She held out a hand and I took it. Han said, "We have exactly one hour."

"I said, "How?"

She said, "Cousin Snood. He's gone up to comfort Mrs. Crowthers. His boat's down the shore. We've got an hour."

I kept holding her hand, and I said, "Mrs. Crowthers said Cousin Snood would come by and she'd find out what happened."

"She knows by now. They lied to me!"

"Who?"

"My mother. She told me you didn't want to see me again. I didn't know if I should come."

"What made you believe I said that?"

"Because I'm supposed to believe my mother."

"She told me you said I was cheap and no good, and you didn't want to have anything to do with me, and that your father was out of his mind at what we'd done. She said to be smart and do as she said."

Then Han began to recite a speech I realized she'd been working on for days. She said Cousin Snood came to tell her the difference, and made her promise to come and tell me what I didn't know. But she said after that, it was her idea. Today was her hot day and her boy day, and we had one hour before Cousin Snood sneaked down the shore to his boat. According to Elzada's books, the moment was at hand.

And according to Elzada's books, Han was going to have my baby all the same. She put on her clothes, went out into the sawmill, and I have not seen Han since. I did hear Cousin Snood put his boat in gear, but only because I was listening. If I hadn't known he was there, I wouldn't have noticed. I didn't bring the subject up, but Han promised me this would be her "only dalliance in a long married life." She said her husband was "all right," and they had married in good faith and she would keep her vows. "Kiss me forever," she had said, and after she was gone I picked up her swim suit and put it on the nail.

Then I walked across to our house, and asked Mrs. Crowthers to make me another Old Crow cup of tea. She said, "Of course! I guess there's enough Old Crow left. Cousin Snood came by and we had an emergency honk."

204

Chapter 53

AND HAN'S
MOTHER

The summer was almost over. It would be a while yet before we'd go to Philadelphia, and the days were long. Mr. and Mrs. Thomas hadn't stayed. Promising to find somebody to take their places, they had made left-handed farewells and sailed off to the Island. Mrs. Thomas made no effort to keep a friendship alive, but Mr. Thomas did. He told my father he'd be around off and on to keep an eye on things and he'd write if anything happened. Then he grinned at my father and said, "I may write even if nothing happens." He said when it came time for us to leave he'd take us to the train if Cousin Snood couldn't do it, and he'd speak to Cousin Snood. He said he was sorry things worked out "this way," and he certainly would look in on us in summers to come.

It was a lonely goodbye. Without Han and the old ways none of us seemed to have any great interest in Morning River Farm. And none of us, not even I, had known how much Han meant to Morning River, and I knew it only after she was gone.

I walked up the river one day, just for something to do, and on my way back stepped across and went into the Croze Nest. Mrs. Thomas was there, as before, sitting on the bunkbed and waiting for me. I didn't expect her, but I knew she was coming one day to gather up some things at the Marcoux house. Mr. Thomas, with an errand at Port Clyde, would return later.

I closed the door behind me and stood still.

Mrs. Thomas said, "Aren't you going to say hello?"

"Hello."

"That's better. Hello."

I had a few fall asters in my hand, and I stepped over to put them in the vase Han always took care of. Mrs. Thomas said, "They're early this year."

"Yes."

She patted the bunk-bed again, as I remembered she did before, but I couldn't think of any news she might have that would thrill me. She said, "Come here; I've got to tell you something."

I did go over and I sat down, but not cozy. How could I love Han so very much and detest her mother?

Now Mrs. Thomas reached to take my hand, and she pulled my hand towards her until my palm was flat against her stomach. She moved my hand in a circle on her belly. "This is it," she said.

"What?"

Mrs. Thomas said, "Oh, my God!"

And she said, "I'm just trying to tell you that you and I are going to have a baby!"

If silence is golden, Mrs. Thomas sat in extreme wealth, and I added more and more every second. She said, "You numb gorm!" She left the Croze Nest and waited on the wharf until Mr. Thomas came, and then they loaded some things on the sloop and left. I never saw either again, but even after these many years I still get a letter now and then from him. He tells me about his son.

Chapter 53

HAN'S LETTER WITH A FRINGED GENTIAN

We'd been back from Morning River Farm perhaps a month and the tension from the dramatic end of our summer was somewhat eased. But my father and my mother, and Mrs. Crowthers, didn't know much about how Han had been deceived. I think they thought to spare me and didn't ask questions. Cousin Snood, the only person who knew, could have told Mrs. Crowthers that Han came to see me again in our Croze Nest, but I soon realized that he hadn't. I knew I would never tell anybody. And I very well knew that without Han there could never again be any Morning River. Then I came home from school in the afternoon, and Mrs. Crowthers said, "There's a letter for you on the hall stand; it's from Han."

I must have revealed something, because she added, "It's from Monhegan, with Han's writing."

I stood by Mrs. Crowthers as I opened the letter, and it wasn't much of a letter. It was postmarked Monhegan Island, and the cancellation stamp had been thumped with care so it was clear. When I had thought I might be a great postage stamp collector, I used to get mad at postal clerks for sloppy stamp banging so I couldn't read the town name. Now I thought, "Good for Monhegan!" Inside the envelope there was some toilet tissue wrapped around a single bloom of fringed gentian, and a three by five ruled index card with a date on it. Other than that, no message from Han. The gentian was wilted, and the postal service had done it no great good. Mrs. Crowthers sniffed the blossom and said, "Ah."

A gentian offers no abundance of perfume, and less after three days in the mail. But the blue-blue-blue of the island gentian was just as Han had told me it would be—back that day when Han and I had climbed to the top of Monhegan to eat our lunch with the seagulls and to chimpanzeeses the freighter.

Han had told me that day that sometime we'd be back, when the gentians were in flower on Monhegan, which is the only place in the world and the only time that you can see the blue of God's great sky in two directions at once. You can look up, and see it in Monhegan's October sky, and you can look down and see it in the fringed gentians at your feet. The same blue. Han had been up to pick me a gentian. But the date she had written on that index card was not an October date, when Monhegan gentian are blue under the blue Monhegan sky.

It was a date back in August, when I was still at Morning River Farm. It was before we left for Philadelphia.

It was the date when Han and I had just an hour together in our Croze Nest, the date Cousin Snood had dissembled by honking with Mrs. Crowthers. Beside that date on the card, Han had written, "Thank you."

Chapter 54

DAVID
AND
ANDREW

My father had the most wonderful letter from Mr. Thomas about the sloop. It thanked him for the work done by Mr. Dernley, which had been paid for promptly by a Winnifred Loomis, unknown to him. The work had been done promptly and the sloop was as good as new. He was not about to get sentimental and gurgle gratitude, but his feelings were warm and permanent, and my father very well knew how he felt. He said that from time to time he would write with information about himself and family, and would continue to keep his eye on the Morning River property and tell how things went. He planned on continuing to bring his Sunday clam-bake people to Morning River, and assumed it would be agreeable if he removed the old one, which was beyond repair, and build a new backhouse in the bushes behind the sawmill, for the convenience of his clam-bake customers. The winter had been holding off, and he hoped to get the new privy in place before snow piled up. Meantime, he had his traps ready and the sloop was waiting to start fishing on Trap Day.

His son-in-law, he said, would continue to lobster from his own boat, but they were considering going together the next season, and if this worked out the sloop would be just for the clam-bakes, with which his son-in-law would help him.

The two ladies, he said, had the first ride in the new sloop, which was now named *Morningstar*, when he took them to Wiscasset to see the doctor that he couldn't spell. The baby doctor. This doctor, lacking a hospital, had a house he used for his baby cases, and had a nurse who lived there and was always ready. Both the "girls" were in good shape and the doctor expected no complications. He couldn't be sure this soon, but he expected both girls would have boys.

Since my father knew nothing about the situation with Mrs. Thomas, the letter was ambiguous at this point, and he and my mother kept trying to guess who this other "girl" might be. Mrs. Crowthers joined in the conundrum, and I lay low and say nuffin. Inwardly, I was churning with constant anxiety over Han, but there seemed to be something to smile about whenever I gave a fleeting thought to Mrs. Thomas. Mr. Thomas was going to get his Piss Against the Wall, and I couldn't very well tell that to my father.

In another letter Mr. Thomas said his son-in-law was a good boy and another season they'd go snacks in his power boat. He was making Han a good husband, which I found was a good thing to know. Also, they would work together in off-season with the clam bakes, and they were putting a small advertisement in the Bangor paper. The backhouse was finished and installed, the first all-new building at Morning River Farm since 1624. Cousin Snood had a compass saw, and he had cut a crescent and star. No mention of Han in that letter.

But in his next letter he said Han was fine, and she would lanch off the carbide saluting cannon when the *Morningstar* set out Sundays for a clam bake. He said Cousin Snood spent a hundred dollars in mileage and time to find some carbide, which cost ten cents at any store when he was a kid, and was used to make acetylene gas for bicycle lamps. He said it was great fun when the party sailed and everybody on the island stepped out when the gun went off and waved. On Fourth of July, he wrote, Han shot the cannon when they put up the post office flag. The post office wasn't open on the Fourth of July, so they had to make believe. And everybody stepped out, but there was no *Morningstar* clam-bake that day, either.

In another letter he told about laying a pipe from the river so it flushed the new toilet. The water ran all the time, so there was no tank of water and no lever to move. Mr. Thomas doubted if the running water would freeze in the winter, and later he wrote that it didn't.

The next summer I took some special classes, getting ready for college and law school, and I didn't go to Morning River. I didn't want to go, anyway, as it would mean being near Han, and her mother, whether I saw them or not, and Mr. Thomas had written that he planned to use the Marcoux House when Han and her mother came back from Wiscasset. So I stayed in Philadelphia. So did my mother and father, and so did Mrs. Crowthers. Mrs. Crowthers really wanted to go. Her purpose was to beat up Cousin Snood, who had been telling everybody that he and Mrs. Crowthers had spent the winter in the Bahamas. Mrs. Crowthers didn't know this until Mr. Thomas mentioned it in a letter to my father.

The year that the two boys were going-on two, my father and mother, and Mrs. Crowthers, were at Morning River and started a new era. Winnifred found that a small float-plane pilot was offering taxi service along the Maine coast, and was pond-hopping in the woodlands. He was ready to pick up passengers in the Kennebec River in Bath, and for us, land them at our estuary at Morning River. Mrs. Crowthers was petrified. "You'll never get me in any flying machine," she said. When the train got to Bath that morning, the plane was waiting, and the pilot and his helper got the baggage loaded, had my mother and father in their seats, and gave their attention to the uncooperative Mrs. Crowthers, poised for flight. "NOW!" said the pilot, and Mrs. Crowthers landed unceremoniously on the cushions, a scream stuck in her throat and her backside uncouthly abused. Before Mrs. Crowthers could make a sound the plane was airborne and past Hell Gate, and Mrs. Crowthers was the world's foremost booster for air travel. "The only way to go!" she kept saying.

And, in mere minutes, everybody was ashore at Morning River Farm, and as the plane took off on return Cousin Snood's power boat came into sight to the west'ard and he was agreeably surprised to find anybody was about.

But it was sad all around, just the same. I wasn't there, and there would be many years ahead when I wouldn't be, or would be for just a short time. I never did see Han at Morning river again, and I purposely avoided it. She did come and always had the two boys with her. Cousin Snood frequently brought her by, but her husband did, too. I wondered if her husband was ever in the Croze Nest? Was Mrs. Thomas ever in the Croze Nest again?

Many questions; few answers. I did notice that Han's bathing suit was still on that nail many years later, and perhaps is still there. The beautiful spy glass was there, too, covered with its cloth but ever ready to look again at Spain, or a ketch passing through. But our Morning River Farm is today still there, and is not unused year to year. Mr. Thomas continued to keep his eye on things, and he writes good letters frequently. The boys, he says, are growing fast, and go with him in the *Morningstar*. They look so much alike, and being of an age, he has trouble telling them apart, David from Andrew, his son and his grandson. "Amazing likeness," he writes. Named, he said, for his two brothers, who never grew up. Drowned in Lobster Cove as youngsters. David and Andrew. David and Andrew, my sons, belong.

But I'm from away.